Where the Sky Meets the Sea

Kit Barrie

Content Warning

This novel contains descriptions of hunting and killing of large sea creatures, drugging for purposes of kidnapping, violence, and talk of enslavement, experimentation, and genocide. It also contains explicit consensual sexual situations and is not intended for children.

Chapter 1

THE SUN WAS JUST rising at the edge of the sky, bathing the sea in shimmering white and gold. The waves were small and not very rough, and there was hardly any wind for the airship to fight against. Perfect weather for whall hunting.

Eron Marcel stood on the deck of the airship SERENITY, looking down across the water with a pair of bi-oculars, searching for the telltale whoosh of sea spray that indicated a whall coming to the surface. The airship crew had spotted several in the area yesterday, but it had been too late to chase after them before darkness fell. Going after whalls in the dark was a fool's errand, and Captain Lavinia Byron, the captain of the SERENITY, was no fool.

Whalls were big creatures, sixty feet or more for the largest ones, and while they had gills to breathe underwater for extended periods, they came to the surface every few hours to expel the waste the sea water created. That was when the sky divers would strike.

"Anything yet?" came a call from across the deck. His best friend, Laurisse Wickham, stood on the other side, his own bi-oculars trained on the glittering waves.

"No," Eron replied. Laurisse was suddenly next to him, sighing dramatically and flopping against Eron.

"I don't know how you can stand this. It's so boring," he lamented.

Eron rolled his eyes and gave Risse a shove. "It's just like fishing."

Risse wrinkled his nose. "You say that like I have ever been fishing in my life. There has to be a better way to do this." He sighed loudly and shoved his hand through his braided hair that was tied back.

"You're the inventor," Eron pointed out.

Risse was an engineer, rarely sitting still. He was always building or designing something. He was not an experienced whall hunter like Eron was. Whall hunting had just been the quickest job Risse had been able to find after his life imploded in spectacular fashion a few weeks ago. Eron had warned Risse that moving in with his partner, who also happened to be his boss at his factory job, was a terrible idea. But after a nasty argument, being thrown out of the apartment, and fired from his job at the same time, there had been no 'I told you so.' Eron had just let his best friend come stay with him and had gotten him a job on his whalling crew until Risse could get his life put back together. Risse was taking advantage of it to study airships and some of their components, but Eron could tell that he was looking forward to getting back on land and finding another job more suited to his skills. Sky diving was a lot of 'hurry up and wait,' and Risse was not a 'hurry up and wait' kind of person, especially compared to Eron.

Sky diving was not for everyone. It was one of the few jobs in Port Ceyran that made a decent amount of money, but there was also so much danger involved that, for many people, it was not worth the risk. Sky divers spent most of their time on airships, searching for whalls, and then hauling their prize back to Port Ceyran after they succeeded in their hunt. They were rarely home and did not know when, or even if, they might return.

In addition to the danger of hunting the powerful whalls, there were all kinds of creatures deep in the dark water, some with massively large teeth, some with grasping tentacles and crushing beaks, some of whom could swamp their retrieval boat like it was no more than tissue paper. It was why most people did not stay in whalling longer than a few years and why the mortality rate was so high.

Eron had lost a number of friends over the seven years he had been a sky diver. He had earned his First-Class rating two years ago, after five years of sky diving. Now, at age twenty-seven, he was still at it. For how much longer, he was not sure, but as a sky diver, he lived day to day, and that was the best he could ask for.

Risse sighed and slumped against the railing, sliding his gloved fingers over one of the many ropes tethering the vessel to the large balloon that kept the airship in the sky. "I don't feel like an inventor much anymore. Things are so shitty out there, man."

Eron gave his friend a nudge in the shoulder with his fist. "Hey. It will get better. After this hunt, you'll be able to afford your own place, and then you'll get another job." He wouldn't have minded Risse staying with him, but his tiny apartment was not big enough for the two of them during the time Eron was home, with no room for Risse to do the inventing work he enjoyed. And frankly, Eron's apartment had seen better days about a decade ago and never recovered. It was a place off the streets when he was not on the SERENITY, though only marginally better than some of the seedy hotels in the red-light district only a few streets away.

"Whall to starboard!" came a call from further down the airship deck, and Eron glanced up to see Kristia Llewellyn, the crew's first mate, standing at the aft of the ship, bi-oculars trained on something below her. Eron took off running to his station, and Risse reluctantly followed.

There were multiple harpoon launchers along the railing of the SERENITY. Some airships preferred gatling guns, but Captain Byron wanted the hide to remain as undamaged as possible, which would earn them more profit. Eron preferred harpoons anyway. There was something unsporting about hunting with a gun versus a harpoon that took more skill and effort to use.

There was a faint *whoosh* from below, barely heard over the lap of the waves and thrum of the airship engine, and Eron spotted the spray of water at the surface. It was a large whall, over fifty feet, and his heart gave a leap of excitement. Bigger whalls were more of a challenge, and they ultimately brought in more profit once they were returned to the port to be processed.

Crew members darted around him, and Eron took up his position at one of the harpoon launchers. Risse stood behind him, another harpoon in hand to load once the first one had been released.

Captain Byron stood on the upper deck to pilot the ship while Kristia called out coordinates. Eron had been working with them for almost three years now. It was a testament to Lavinia Byron's skills that she had been captaining the SERENITY for almost nine years. In her late thirties, she was one of the oldest active sky divers that Eron knew, though she more often steered the ship than fired the harpoons or went out in the retrieval boat anymore since Kristia had come aboard. Kristia was twenty-four, with a cherubic face framed by chestnut ringlets, her diving goggles perched on her head. Risse had once described the ambitious young woman as "little but fierce," and Eron had to whole-heartedly agree. Only recently promoted to first mate, Kristia was eager to prove to Captain Byron that she had what it took to take over as captain when Captain Byron retired. "Gunners ready!" Kristia barked in a voice much bigger than her tiny frame would suggest.

The airship began to dip. They had to get low enough that they could launch the harpoons, but landing on the water would not be a good idea until they brought the whall down. The hunting vessels were designed for both air and water, and while on the ocean, they pulled in seawater to pump through the engines to create the steam that powered the mighty craft for flight. But a flailing whall could damage an airship in many ways, and a damaged airship meant a slower return to the port and repairs, which meant lost time, lost wages, and less usable whall if the creature degraded too much on the return journey.

The airship turned, and Eron kept his launcher focused on the spout of water below, his heart beating rapidly in his chest. "Ready and hold," Kristia called, surveying the distance with her bi-oculars. Eron cocked back the trigger mechanism, double-checking that neither he nor Risse were in the path of the rope attached to the harpoon.

Kristia jumped up on the railing of the airship, and Eron couldn't stop a flinch. No matter how many times she did that, it still worried him. She had no fear when it came to heights, which was sometimes helpful, but it also seemed reckless with all of the time they spent hundreds of feet above the sea. Falling and hitting the water at that distance was a death sentence for sure. Kristia held onto a rope line with one hand while crouching to watch the sea get closer and closer. "Hold," she called again, though her voice was rising in the pitch that told Eron they were almost ready.

The ship banked again. "Fire!" Kristia called, and Eron loosed the harpoon from the launcher with an unmistakable twang.

The harpoon soared downward at the angle Eron had launched it, a tie line attached to it whipping behind it like the string of a kite. "Gotcha," Eron whispered to himself.

The harpoon struck true, and the whall surged up out of the water with a bellow that cut through the air like a crack of thunder. More crew members loosed harpoons, and one slammed into the whall's side. The creature rolled, and Eron swore under his breath, hitting the release. If the whall did not roll, the harpoons were easily retrieved once they had attached the whall to the airship to bring it back to the city. But when they did roll, the harpoons had to be released right away, or the whall could drag the airship down. The whall twisted again, and the next crew member's harpoon shot went wide, striking into the water a few feet away. But Eron and Risse had already loaded another harpoon into the launcher and set it. Eron loosed it, and this one flew straight, hitting the top of the whall's head with a hollow sound that set his teeth on edge.

The whall splashed back into the water, flailing and bellowing, but Eron could see it was flagging fast. "Divers to the boat," Kristia called.

Eron turned to Risse. "Come one. Last one, I promise."

Risse sighed and nodded, pulling his goggles down over his eyes. "Can't wait," he grumbled.

Eron pulled his own goggles on as he, Risse, and four other crew members headed for the retrieval boat. Attached to the side of the airship, it functioned as both the boat for the divers to reach the downed whall and also could function as a lifeboat in the event of an airship emergency. Eron was lucky he had not ever had that happen in his career. He hopped over the side of the airship into the smaller boat, but Risse used the ladder, clinging to it so tightly that Eron was sure his knuckles were white under his leather gloves.

Once all six were aboard, the retrieval boat began to lower until it hung about ten feet below the bottom of the airship. Eron adjusted his goggles over his eyes as he slid his dive gear on. Over his clothes and boots he pulled on a fitted diving suit, ironically made of whall hide. It slid over his entire body, from feet to neck, secured in place with various buckles and latches. His oxygen tank was strapped to his back, and he held his helmet on his lap until he was ready to dive. The helmet was mostly to keep the water out; there was an aircap attached to his tank that went inside of the helmet that provided oxygen for him. The sky divers often had to swim under the whall to free the harpoons or to get the whall into a better position for towing. That was the part he hated about whalling, going into the dark, murky water. One never knew what waited for them just below the surface.

The SERENITY dipped further, the sound of the whall's splashing and lowing growing steadily quieter, until the retrieval boat touched the water, and the lines holding it slackened. The crew released the mooring hooks that held it to the airship, untethering it and leaving it bobbing on the surface of the vast ocean. Once the retrieval boat was freed, the airship began to slowly ascend again, though not as high as before, as it waited.

The retrieval boat surged forward, its gas motor filled with whall oil propelling it along the waves toward the whall that floated on the surface, harpoons and ropes sticking out of it like some sort of grotesque monument.

"That's a big'un," said William at the front, spitting a mouthful of tobacco juice over the side of the boat. "What do ya think, Marcel, fifty feet?"

"Fifty-seven," Eron replied with a grin.

"Naw, not more than fifty-one," William said.

"I'll bet you five Struck it's over fifty-five," Eron replied.

William smirked. "You're on."

"I'm with Eron, I think it's at least fifty-five," said Marimore next to him, and the conversation devolved into a playful argument between the two.

Next to Eron, Risse was sweating in his own gear, scrunching his nose is disgust at the smell of blood and other things emanating from the whall's body. Eron patted his shoulder reassuringly. "Almost done, Risse. Just get through this one, and then we'll go home."

"I swear that thing moved," Risse said, sounding more than a little trepidatious as he fiddled with the strap of his tank.

"Get it together, Wick," laughed Isaiah Cameron from further at the front. "It's dead."

"I'm telling you, it's not," Risse said, casting a helpless glance back at Eron. "It's playing possum."

Eron stared at the whall bobbing on the surface for a moment. It seemed like its gills were flaring a little, out of the water as they were, but that wasn't unusual. It was also possible that there was something in the water that was nibbling at the creature. He hoped that was not the case. He really did not feeling like losing part of their catch to one of the razor-toothed sharks. "They don't do that. It's close to dead, Risse," he reassured his friend as the boat drew nearer.

Risse shot him a stormy look, and Eron pretended to adjust his own tank so he did not have to meet his best friend's gaze. Risse was inexperienced, but he was not dumb. And Eron did not fault him for being concerned. This whall was big, but they had speared it true, and it had wrapped itself up well with the ropes. And while whalls were not completely illogical creatures, he had yet to ever have one play dead in the seven years he had been hunting.

A few feet from the giant animal, the retrieval boat slowed, and William and Marimore slid into the water. If their harpoons were secure enough, they could be left in place until they returned to the port, using the ropes and harpoons to tow. Of course, towing was not the safest part of the journey either; more than one whall had been lost by deep sea creatures latching onto it for a meal and nearly dragging the ship under the waves. Losing their quarry after all of their hard work might not even be the worst part. The vessel was designed to sail on water like any other ship, but it would also capsize just as easily in the sky or on the sea if enough strength was applied.

Risse let out a sharp breath. "Eron, man, I'm telling you, it's not dead."

Eron adjusted his goggles, then reached for his helmet. "Risse, it's fine. Nothing is-"

His words were cut off as the whall's tail, which had not yet been restrained, suddenly rose up, blocking out the sunlight for a moment, before it came smashing down in a massive splash of water. The retrieval boat spun, pitching Isaiah off of it with a shout. Eron reached to try to grab him, but the sun was suddenly blotted out again, much longer this time, and Eron gasped as the massive body of the whall surged up and then came slamming back down.

There was a sickening crunch and the crack of wood splintering, and Eron felt his stomach rise as the world suddenly tipped sideways, the bench of the boat gone from beneath him. He barely had time to take a breath before his back slammed into the cold waves, and dark water surged over his head. Eron was thankful for his diving goggles so he could still see, making out light above him. He flung himself toward it, almost to the surface, when something large, maybe part of the retrieval boat, smashed into the water right above him. The force drove him back down under the surface as the large thing blotted out the light and sent him tumbling head over heels in the icy, churning depths. His body struggled to right itself, but he realized in a panic that he had no idea which way the surface was, the water around him dark and churning, full of movement and bubbles and debris.

Something struck him across the side of the head, knocking his diving goggles and aircap from his face and sending spots darker than the water dancing in front of his eyes. The salt water stung as it filled his nose and mouth, and he felt panic surge into his chest as he desperately groped in the murky water for the aircap. And then he felt his tank loosen and fall off his shoulders, making him suddenly much lighter even as his heart grew as heavy as iron.

Find the surface, or grab for his air tank? Which one gave him the better chance for survival in this moment? He was so panicked, he couldn't even decide. He couldn't see his tank, and the water was moving so much, it was impossible to see where it had fallen or even how deep the water was. *Find the surface!* his brain screamed at him, and he squinted, desperately looking for any sign of light or movement that indicated which way was up. The water around him was filled with pieces of wood and metal, stinging eyes and the murky darkness making it even more difficult to see anything beyond his own hand. If he did not find the surface, he was not going to make it. His lungs were already screaming for air. He saw a flash of white and surged for it, hoping his instincts were right and that it was sunlight. His body felt so heavy, the weight of his own limbs dragging him back as he tried to move. He needed to breathe so badly, the corners of his vision starting to go dark. The brightness he had seen had vanished.

Everything went strangely silent around him, and Eron could not make out anything in the water now. No light, no sound, no movement, just eerie stillness. This was it. This was how he died. Trapped underwater, nothing around him but empty, cold nothingness. Was that what death was too? Just nothing? His lungs were burning, his whole body so heavy he could not even move it. He closed his eyes. Just breathe in the water, it would be over soon.

Something pressed to his mouth, and warm air rushed into his lungs, filling them up. There was death, so soft and reassuring, taking him down into the blackness. He let it.

Chapter 2

HE STARTED COUGHING BEFORE he had even opened his eyes, lungs and gullet burning, feeling like he was trying to breathe through a wet sponge. Eron retched, tasting bile and slimy sea water in his throat and over his tongue before he spat it out, coughing harder. Whatever he was curled up on was rough and cold. When he opened his eyes, his dark hair was hanging in them, and he brushed it away with a hand that was equally wet. He was lying on his front, so he tried to push himself onto his side. He was cold, so very cold, and he felt like he weighed a thousand pounds. He gazed blearily down at himself; he could see he was still in his diving suit. His clothes under it were wet, having been flooded without his helmet to seal it.

He sat up, his arms shaking, though from cold or something else, he was not sure. His teeth chattered, and he wrapped his arms around himself as he tried to bring his stinging eyes into focus. He was inside something with stone walls. A cavern, perhaps? He was sitting on a stony embankment that was plenty wide for him, but a few feet away, it fell off into a pool of water. Sea water, from the smell of it. The whole area smelled briny and damp. His hair dangled into his gray eyes again, and he shoved it back, trying to wring out some of the water to keep it from falling again. He coughed, stomach surging, and he doubled over, retching sea water again until he felt boneless and light-headed.

Once the retching had stopped, and it felt like his breath was returning to him, Eron pushed himself into a sitting position again, curling his legs up to his chest as he looked around. He was not too far from the entrance of the cave, and he could see bright afternoon sunlight and blue sky through the rocks, as well as lightly lapping sea waves. The water made a little inlet path from outside the cavern to inside where he was, though he could not see how deep it was anywhere.

Something was poking out of the dark water, barely visible through the ripples, only because it was lighter. A flop of blond hair. Eron rubbed at his eyes that were still stinging, noting his missing goggles. He looked again, but the light spot was still in the water nearby, and it definitely bobbed like hair. But that couldn't be, unless another of his sky divers had come this way too. But none of them had strawberry blond hair like that, he was sure. And, as the waves sloshed, he thought he saw something beneath them. Eyes? He blinked, and the things blinked back. Definitely eyes. He gasped sharply, drawing his legs in further as he stared.

The hair and eyes lifted from the water, and Eron realized with a start that whatever the creature was, it was vaguely humanoid, with a head on a slender neck attached to shoulders that was not much different in structure from his own. The face was delicately curved, with a human-like nose and lips, slender cheeks, and a petite chin. Eron couldn't tell right away if the creature was male or female, but whatever it was, its face was lovely. Long, light lashes framed its eyes, the irises a gleaming golden amber, almost orange, with a dark, perfectly round pupil in the center.

The head tipped curiously to one side, regarding him, and Eron saw with a start that rather than ears on the sides of its head, there were what looked like fins instead, with a firmer structure and a strange, almost delicate webbing between them, like the fin on the spine of a fish. The ear fins perked up, seeming to move almost of their own accord, and Eron sucked in a sharp breath. The ear fins twitched at the sound. It was such a strange movement that he might have laughed if he had not been so terrified.

The eyes gazed at him for a long moment, and Eron did not look away, as if to do so would bring the creature charging forward. The staring contest between them stretched for he couldn't tell how long before the water rippled, and the creature appeared to be coming closer. But the movement was slow and cautious, the golden eyes bright and full of something he couldn't decipher, but it didn't seem malicious. He stayed still where he was, legs pulled in defensively, body tight if he needed to dive aside.

The creature stopped a few yards away, continuing to stare at him with unblinking eyes. A long, lean arm came out of the water to rest on the edge of the stones, and Eron saw that there was that fin-like webbing in between each finger on the four-fingered hand. Well, three fingers and a thumb, he realized. *That's interesting, a water creature that has thumbs,* he vaguely thought in the back of his head, not sure where that had even come from.

The creature seemed to hesitate for a moment before a second arm emerged, and it slowly pulled itself out of the water and onto the stony ledge. Eron could not stop a gasp of surprise that was shockingly loud in the rocky enclosure.

The creature was not very large. In fact, he was pretty sure that stretched out side by side, he would have been taller than it by at least a few inches, if not more. The chest was sculpted similar to his own, the pecs a little more rounded and muscular. Not quite breasts, and he realized with slight curiosity that there were no nipples on the chest. Down the torso was a well-defined upper abdomen, but where the stomach and navel were, the creature's shape and color began to shift. Almost like the ombre of a sunset, the creature's light skin began to shimmer with bits of blue, almost the same color as the ocean when viewed from the sky. And by the time it reached where its groin would be, the body was fused into a single long tail, like a fish or a whall, that ended with pointed, webbed fins not unlike its ears. There appeared to be scales all over its tail that shimmered in the light coming from the grotto entrance. The scales were a dark blue with hints of green, the color changing a little with the play of the light across them, and Eron was not surprised that he had not been able to make out the fishy-looking half while the creature was in the water. It looked like its skin was designed to help it blend in with the sea's darkness. There was no apparent genitalia anywhere; Eron vaguely thought he might have felt extremely awkward if there was, since he realized he had been looking for it.

The fish creature continued to stare at him for a long time, and Eron stared back. If the creature was going to attack him, it was certainly taking its time about it. But the almost human-like face didn't look like that of a predator. The bright eyes and flickering ear fins seemed… curious? Eron cautiously untensed his legs, shifting into a less vulnerable position. The creature stirred just a bit, like it was preparing to jump back in the water if needed. Eron froze again, waiting, and the creature continued to just gaze at him.

Eron licked his lips that were surprisingly dry compared to the rest of him, tasting the briny salt there. "Hello," he said, keeping his voice low and soft, like he was addressing a small child.

The creature blinked but otherwise did not move.

"Can you speak?" Eron asked.

The creature cocked its head, the blue fin protrusions on its temples flicking back and forth a little. It seemed like it could hear him, at least, so that was good, right?

Eron pointed to himself. "Eron," he said.

The ear fins flicked again.

"Eron," Eron repeated, then pointed at the creature. "What is your name?"

The creature slid back just a little as Eron's hand moved, still keeping out of Eron's reach.

Eron pulled his hand back. "Sorry," he said, and the ear fins shook a bit. "Can you talk?"

The creature regarded him for a moment, tipping its head to the other side like a curious animal. Eron sighed. "Probably not," he muttered. That was so not helpful right now.

The creature's mouth suddenly opened, and Eron jerked back as he saw that the creature's visible teeth were conical. His hands went up, wondering if the creature was about to attack him, but the creature stayed where it was, and a clicking sound suddenly filled the air. It took a moment for him to hear it over the rush of his heart in his ears. He wasn't sure what he was hearing, but it seemed to be coming from the creature in front of him. A form of communication, perhaps?

The clicking stopped, and the creature closed its mouth, gazing back at him with that same curious look. Eron frowned slightly. "Was that you?"

The creature's ear fins flicked back and forth again.

"Are you going to eat me?"

The creature stared at him, seemingly uncomprehending. Eron hesitated a moment, then slowly lifted up his hands in a show of peace. "I won't hurt you if you don't hurt me," he said. "Deal?"

The creature blinked, but its ear fins moved again, and Eron decided that was probably a good sign. He realized how cold and wet he still was. He glanced down at his dive suit that was clinging to him in very odd ways because of his wet clothes, and his teeth started to chatter. He wrapped his arms around himself and curled his legs tightly to his chest, trying to maintain his body heat. Where was his team? For that matter, where was he? He looked around the rocky cavern again. There seemed to only be one entrance, behind the fish creature, and he doubted that he could have easily come along that passage and ended up on the rocks on his own with barely a scratch. "Did... Did you save me?" he asked.

The creature's ears flicked again. Eron gave it a weak smile through his shivers. "Thank you."

There did not seem to be anyone else around, human or otherwise. Eron felt a lump in his throat that he quickly swallowed back. Risse had been right. The whall had been alive, perhaps biding its time until the retrieval boat was close enough for it to broadside. He groaned, rubbing at his face for a moment with his hand. Was Risse still alive? The rest of the crew? Would the airship have been able to retrieve them from the water before anyone else lost their gear or became trapped?

The creature was still watching him, and Eron wrapped his arms tighter, which only pressed the wet clothing more onto his chilled skin. "Cold," he said in response to the curious look the creature gave him.

The creature blinked, as if not sure what he had said, before it suddenly slid off the rocky ledge and into the water with a graceful and surprisingly quiet splash. It disappeared under the surface, vanishing from his view, and Eron stared at where it had gone. Had he done something to offend it or scare it?

The sound of something breaking the water's surface came from behind him, and Eron shifted to see that the grotto went back further still, with a sort of rocky outcropping at the back. The fish creature had come out of the water and was looking at Eron expectantly.

"What?" Eron asked, and the creature's ear fins flickered, giving him a pointed look. "Do you want me to come over there?"

The fins flicked again, and Eron slowly got to his feet. His body hurt all over, like he had been wrestling and slammed into the floor a few times, but everything at least felt intact, nothing broken or sprained. He realized in the dim light that the rocky ledge he was on went all the way to the back so he would not have to get in the water again, and for that he was profoundly grateful as his clothes dripped water inside his suit with every step. He carefully picked his way over the rocks, which were slick with sea spray, until he reached the wider platform area. Now he could see that there was a litany of objects scattered around, some in haphazard piles, nothing seeming to have a particular reason for its location.

The creature picked up something and held it out to him. Eron blinked. It was a wrench, the same type used by most factories and airships. He took it, and the creature gave him what seemed to be an excited smile, ear fins fluttering. Eron glanced at it, then over at the fish creature. "What is this for?"

The creature stared at him, then wrapped its arms around its torso in an imitation of Eron. "Oh," he said. "This is a wrench. It doesn't help with cold." He held it back out. The creature took it, seeming disappointed, and put it aside before sliding across the slick stones to grab something else and come back to him. This time it held out what appeared to be an empty cut glass jar of some sort of face cream. Eron shook his head again. "That doesn't help either."

The creature let out a huff and put the jar down. Eron glanced around. There were probably hundreds of objects scattered over the whole area. If the creature decided to bring everything to him individually, they'd be at this all day and night. And, he realized with a start, the cave was growing dimmer. The sun was setting, and the cave was gradually losing light. "Can I look around?" he asked the creature, motioning to the piles. The creature blinked, then flicked its ear fins in assent.

Eron frowned, trying to make out what some of the shapes were in the dimness. He saw what might have been a pile of fabric and started for it, then heard something crunch under his boot. He flinched, looking over at the creature, who just stared back at him curiously, not seeming to be concerned about whatever he had just done. He lifted his foot to see that it had been nothing more than one of the lenses from a broken bi-ocular, and he breathed a sigh of relief it hadn't been anything precious or alive. "Sorry," he said to the fish creature, who just blinked at him. Eron took that to mean that his destruction was not a concern. His boots squelched as he walked; he wondered if they would ever be dry again.

He glanced around, and then spotted a slightly familiar lump underneath a coil of rope. It was a sky diver pack. Not one he recognized, so it was probably from a different diver crew, but it would probably have very similar items to his own, and potentially even food and water. He moved over to it, shifting the rope and a broken piece of pottery aside until he could free the bag. It was heavy, and the buckle holding it closed was still in place. If the creature had brought it here, it had not figured out how to get into it.

He thumbed the buckle carefully open. The material was swollen and discolored from sea water, but it had obviously been here for at least a little while, as it was completely dry inside and out. He reached in, and his heart leaped in delight when he pulled out a steel flask, hearing liquid sloshing inside. Hopefully it was water and not some crew member's homemade gin. He unscrewed the lid and took a cautious sniff, then sighed with relief. He put the flask to his lips and drank several gulps of the water. It tasted old and warm, but he didn't care. He put the lid on when the flask was half-emptied, reminding himself he had no idea where he was or if there was fresh water nearby.

He dug into the pack again and came out with several maps, wrapped in oilskin to protect them from the water. He would look closer at them later. Several basic tools, none of which would help him at the moment, a set of clothes, a small lantern, and, in the bottom, a bag of provisions. Salted and dried meat, wax-wrapped cheese, dried fruit, some nuts. It was not a lot, but it would keep him alive for now.

He shook out the clothing, glad to find a shirt, trousers, socks, and undergarments. He reached up and began to undo the various latches and buckles of his diving suit. The whall skin would at least dry quickly, but he was not so sure about everything under it. He slid the diving suit off his arms and down his legs, stepping out of it. A splash nearby made him look up, and he saw the creature had slid back into the water and was watching him with just its eyes showing above the waterline, like when he had first seen it. He held up the suit for it to see, but the creature just stared. Eron sighed and sat down to undo his boots and pull them off. It was only when he pulled off the second one that he had a stroke of realization. The creature didn't have any clothes on. Eron pulling his wet things off his body probably looked terrifying if the creature didn't know what clothing was. He glanced over to see the creature still watching from under the water, though now its head had fully poked back up. "It's all right," he said, holding up the boot he had just removed. "It's supposed to come off." The creature just stared.

Eron sighed. He was too wet and cold to try to explain clothing further to this creature right now, so he just pulled off his sodden shirt and socks and undid his trousers. He stood up and slid them off, leaving him in just his white undergarment that clung to him in all the wrong places. He started to reach for them, then felt eyes on him. He glanced over at the creature, who was still watching him closely. "Can I have some privacy, please?"

The creature just blinked. Eron sighed again. Fine, he was just going to have to get naked in front of the fish thing. He peeled his underwear from his skin, sliding it off and down his legs before stepping out of them. He was still cold, but it was a relief to not have the wet clothes clinging to his skin anymore. He glanced up at the creature to see it still watching him with those wide, golden eyes. He flushed a bit and turned away, quickly grabbing up a random piece of fabric to use as a towel to wipe himself down as best he could.

Once he was as dry as he could make himself, he scooped up the dry underwear and trousers from the pack and pulled them on, finding a piece of rope nearby to tie around the waist to keep them up. They were definitely made for a much portlier person than he, but the dry fabric felt amazing, if not a bit stiff from the salt water and air. He picked up the shirt, turning it around in his hands before sliding it over his head. It billowed on him like a nightshirt, and he tucked it into his trousers as best he could. There was no waistcoat or jacket. At least he didn't have to worry about looking presentable at the moment. He supposed he could forgo shoes and socks while his boots dried.

Eron turned around, then saw that the creature had come out of the water, so quietly he hadn't heard it over the lap of the waves on the stone, and it was now sitting on the edge of the rocks again, watching him. "Oh, hi." The creature's ear fins flicked. Eron gestured to the dry clothing. "Thank you," he said, not sure if the creature understood him, but it felt appropriate to thank it. He sat down on a clear patch of stone, grabbing the bag of provisions. Apparently almost drowning made one ravenously hungry. He had to resist the urge to stuff the food in his mouth, instead taking a careful bite of the dried meat. It was salty and tough and tasted like it had been in the pack for longer than it should have, but food was food, and he was not about to protest. He chewed carefully, glancing around the cavern again. When he looked back, the fish creature had slid into the water again and drifted over toward the edge of the larger area where he sat. He watched it approach until it reached the edge and pulled itself up on the stones, only a few feet away. The end of its tail floated in the water as it sat and watched him.

Eron took another bite of the meat, and the creature watched him curiously, tipping its head to the side again as it studied him. It was kind of cute, Eron admitted to himself. Like a wide-eyed puppy. He held out the jerky toward it. "Did you want some?"

The creature glanced down at it, then back up at him. Ear fins twitched nervously. Eron almost pulled it back, but the creature suddenly lifted its hand, reaching out with its four webbed fingers to take the proffered meat. One of its fingers brushed Eron's as it did, and he jumped just a little. The skin was damp from the water, but not as cold as he expected it would be. It was soft too, not entirely dissimilar to his own. He let go of the jerky, watching the creature stare at it, then give it a cautious sniff, before putting the entire piece in its mouth. Eron couldn't stop a sputter of laughter, watching its sharp teeth tear easily through the meat, but then it seemed unsure what to do with it, chewing awkwardly like it was a sticky piece of candy. He took a bite of his own from another piece, and the creature watched him as he chewed and swallowed it, then did the same, running its slightly pointed tongue over those strange conical teeth, as if checking if there was still residue stuck in them. Then it said something to him with that strange clicking sound, ear fins flattening a little as it looked reproachfully at him. Eron held out the other piece in his hand, and the creature wrinkled its nose. Eron chuckled. "Sorry. More for me, I guess."

There was still a little light, so he opened the oil packet of papers to see what they contained. A few maps, including the seas around his city of Port Ceyran, an airship schematic for a ship called the NAUTILUS, not unlike his own whalling ship, and a little diary. Eron opened it curiously, finding the first few pages filled with amateur sketches of flowers and sea creatures. He turned another page, then found himself looking at a crude drawing of what appeared to be a creature like the one in front of him. A human face with ear fins, and a torso that became a fish tail with roughly-drawn scales. In the corner of the page was a single word. *Mer?*

Eron had no idea what 'mer' was. He thought maybe he vaguely recognized it as having something to do with the sea. Was this creature in front of him a 'mer?' He had never heard of such a thing even existing, so he supposed 'mer' was as good a term as any for it. He flipped through the rest of the book, but it was blank. He wondered what had happened to the owner of this pack. If his gear had ended up in the ocean, Eron guessed it was nothing good.

The creature (the *mer*, he corrected himself) watched him for another minute or two while he ate and sorted through the papers before it slowly shifted to look around the cavern. It was getting darker, but there was still enough sunlight filtering in to see by. The mer slid itself with its arms and tail a few feet away, sorting through a pile of stuff that Eron couldn't make it out, before returning and holding out something in its hand. It appeared to be a jewelry box with gold leaf and a cloisonne inlay on the top in the shape of some kind of long-legged bird. Eron glanced up at the creature. "It's a jewelry box."

The mer leaned closer, still holding it out. Eron blinked. "For me?" The mer didn't move. Eron slowly reached up and took the box. It was not overly expensive-looking, something that he might have gotten for his sister as a birthday gift, but it was pretty, and the gold leaf shone in the dying sunlight.

As soon as it let go of the box, the mer dove to the other side, grabbing something else and returning to him with a glass bottle with a stopper. Dark liquid sloshed in the bottom, but the label was too washed out from the water to read it. Eron shrugged. "I don't know what's in there, but that's a bottle." The creature handed it to him, then went off in search of another treasure. Eron sighed and put the jewelry box and the bottle down. They were back to this game now...

The mer returned with something else, extending it out to him eagerly. Eron held out his hand and took it. It was a copper tea kettle, battered and dented, missing its lid and handle. The mer blinked, its ear fins giving a slight quiver. Eron sighed. "That's a tea kettle."

The creature sat up a bit, ear fins twitching. Eron blinked at the enthusiastic response. "Tea kettle?" he asked, and the fins flickered wildly. "Do you know what a kettle is?" The mer cocked its head curiously, its ear fins moving again at the word. Eron dipped the kettle into the water and poured it out through the spout. "Kettle." The mer gazed into his face in a way that was slightly disconcerting, ignoring the movement of his hands as its ear fins flickered wildly.

Eron thought for a moment, then said, "Kettle?" The fins shook again, the mer's eyes seeming to light up, and it gave a few curious clicks. "Do you like that word?" he asked, gazing back at the mer. Its face was intent on his, and it gave another click. "Ket?" he said slowly, and the mer's ear fins practically danced on the sides of its head. With the clicking sounds the creature had made, Eron thought that it would make sense that the hard sounds of the 'k' and the 't' would appeal to it or even sound familiar. He set the copper teapot down, then held up his finger and pointed to himself. "Eron," he said, then shifted to point at the creature. "Ket?"

The mer's tail flicked into the air, sending droplets of water scattering. Eron wiped at his face. *Well, that simplifies things a little bit,* he thought. "Ket," he repeated again, and the tail hit the water with an eager splash.

He doubted that was actually Ket's name, but he was not about to start making random clicking sounds himself until he found the right combination. With his luck, he'd probably insult the mer's mother or something, and he could not afford to offend it and risk it leaving him alone in this grotto with no way out. He also realized he needed to stop thinking of the mer as 'it.' There was an intelligence there, with communication and comprehension, even if he didn't understand the language or signals from the ear fins. Ket was obviously not human, but 'animal' seemed even further from reality.

He wished he had paid better attention to how his sister's little girl thought; that seemed like an apt comparison to Ket when it came to communication. He touched his hand to his chest. "Boy," he said. He felt a little foolish putting it in such simple terms; he was twenty-seven, after all, but he supposed it was easier to start with the basics when not speaking the same language.

"Eron. Boy," he said. He pointed at Ket. "Ket. Girl?" Ket's head tipped curiously to the side, a lock of damp, blond hair flopping a bit. "Ket. Boy?" Eron tried again. Ket's ear fins perked up. Whether that was because the word was familiar or because it meant something, Eron wasn't sure, but he realized he was too tired and sore to keep playing Twenty Questions. The light from outside was almost gone; pretty soon the whole cavern would be in complete darkness. He turned to Ket again. "Can I go to sleep?"

Ear fins flicked. Eron made his hands into a pillow to rest his head on them. "Sleep?"

Ket just stared. Eron was going to take that as a yes, as he had no better ideas right now. He grabbed a few pieces of fabric from nearby and folded it into a makeshift sleeping bag on a clear patch of stone, finding another piece to create a sort of pillow. It was going to be very uncomfortable, but there didn't seem to be many other options right now. He laid down and pulled the fabric up, but he found himself staring at Ket, now only silhouetted against the dim entrance, still sitting on the rock and watching him. He debated telling Ket to shove off and leave him alone, but what good would that do? If the mer had wanted to attack him, he was sure he would have done so by now. Eron shifted a little under the blanket, closing his eyes.

Sleep was going to be hard to come by. His mind was too full of thoughts. What had happened to his team? To Risse? Were there other survivors? Where had they ended up? Had the airship rescued them? Was he all alone here in the vast ocean? How close was the nearest bit of land? If he could reach one of the inhabited islands near the mainland, they would be able to communicate with the airships and let Captain Byron know he was alive. Perhaps he was even on one of them now, just in a cave area. He would have to explore in the morning.

He opened his eyes again. Darkness had fallen, but he could just barely make out the glow of Ket's skin, still on the rocks. He had laid down, resting his chin on his arms, but Eron couldn't see if the mer's eyes were open or closed. He groaned and rolled over onto his side, facing away from Ket. He had to get some rest so he could figure things out tomorrow. It took a very long time, but eventually the quiet lapping of the waves overcame him, and he drifted into uneasy sleep.

Chapter 3

When Eron opened his eyes again, the grotto was lighter. The sky that he could see at the cave entrance was fading from a delicate purple into pale pinks and blues. The sun was rising. He shifted and sat up, feeling stiff and achy from both sleeping on the ground and being tossed in the ocean the day before. He brushed a few strands of dark hair out of his face, then pushed the makeshift blanket aside.

Rising to his feet, he looked around, but he seemed to be alone, no Ket or other living creature in sight. He was just checking if his boots had dried when a splash came from nearby, and he looked up to see Ket crawl onto the rocks, holding something in his mouth. Ket leaned down and set the dead fish on the ledge, then looked up at Eron eagerly, like a dog waiting for praise. Eron blinked at the offering with its bulging eyes. "What is that for?"

Ket cocked his head at him, then gave the fish a push with his webbed fingers to move it closer to him. Eron's stomach decided to take that moment to let out a loud growl, and Ket looked amused and slightly delighted, giving the fish another nudge. Eron frowned down at the dead fish. "Am I supposed to eat that?"

Ket's ear fins flicked. Eron tried very hard not to wrinkle his nose. "Thank you, but I can't eat that raw. I'll get sick."

Ket stared uncomprehendingly at him. Eron groaned to himself. How could he explain 'cooking' to a half-fish creature who caught raw fish with his teeth? It was possible there were some cooking elements that still worked scattered amongst the assorted items around him, but damned if he'd be able to easily find it in the chaos. He had to reach civilization, with cooked food and treated water, and he had to do it soon, before he became too weak to do anything else. The meager supplies in the pack would not last very long.

Ket nudged the fish forward again. "No, thank you," Eron said firmly.

Ket looked disappointed, his head hanging a little. *Great,* Eron thought, *now I offended him.* He pointed to the fish, then to Ket. "Do you eat fish?" Ket's ear fins wiggled. Eron reached into his supplies and pulled out a handful of nuts and dried fruit. "How about, you eat it, and I'll eat with you?" He held up his own food to show Ket.

Ket seemed to consider this for a moment before he plopped himself up on the ledge, picking up the fish with his webbed hands. Eron decided to not watch too closely as Ket ripped into the fish with his teeth, seeming to swallow the bites whole, bones and all. The fruit and nuts were not enough to satisfy his hunger, so he allowed himself half of the cheese as well. Ket looked at it curiously but recoiled in apparent disgust when Eron held a piece out to him. He supposed dairy was not in the diet of a sea-dwelling creature.

What exactly is Ket anyway? Eron mused. Surely Ket couldn't be the only one of his kind, but he had never seen anything like the mer before in all the time he'd been a sky diver. But Captain Byron had never mentioned it to the crew, and she was not one to withhold information that they needed to know. But obviously Ket had been in this area, wherever that was, for a long time, judging by the amount and variety of junk scattered about. The pack from the unknown person had contained no names or notes beyond that single descriptor, *mer?*, and he had not heard anything else about half-human and half-fish creatures, so obviously their existence was not widely known. Unfortunately, even though Ket seemed to understand him fairly well, hand gestures could only go so far when it came to an entirely new, unknown species, so most of his questions would have to go unanswered right now.

Once he had eaten and enough light had entered the cave that he felt safe walking along the rock ledge, Eron got to his feet. Ket watched him, then splashed into the water to follow along beside him as Eron picked his way over the damp rocks. He had to be careful with no boots on, but the water seemed to have smoothed out the most jagged bits of stone. Eron made his way forward, the entrance growing larger and larger as he approached. The walkable ledge stopped a few feet from the entrance, enough that he could not see out. Eron sighed and stripped off his clothing before sliding down into the cold water, doing his best to stay afloat without any gear. Ket was suddenly next to him, and Eron jumped. Ket let out a chirping sound that almost sounded like a giggle, suddenly flipping under the water and splashing Eron with his tail. Eron sputtered and swiped at his face. "Hey, cut that out!"

Ket's head popped up again next to him, looking slightly mopey. Eron sighed. "Sorry. I just need to see where I am." Ket tipped his head, and Eron decided that was a good enough answer, swimming a few strokes and pulling himself up to the cave entrance with his arms before emerging into the sunlight and the open sea.

The waves stretched endlessly before him, and Eron kept a hand on the rocks as he shifted to look around. He hoped he would turn and see vegetation, but the only thing that greeted him was more rock. It was not very high or very wide, probably just a little stone outcropping that had once been under the water and now lay exposed. A few other similar crags jutted up from the water nearby, but there was no land as far as he could see in any direction, and the sky was free of airships. "Fucking hell," he groaned softly.

Something warm brushed against his back, and he nearly leaped out of his skin. Ket splashed backward, ear fins flattened in what looked like apology. Eron's heart raced, and he was suddenly very aware that he could not see into the watery depths beneath him. Perhaps even now, something swam in the darkness, seeing his legs moving and thinking about making him into breakfast. He had no weapons to fight with, for the little good it would do against the monstrous creatures of the deep. With that thought, he quickly swam back along the channel and hauled himself up onto the rocks inside the grotto. He snatched up his clothing and moved along the ledge until he was back at his makeshift camp. He wiped himself off with a piece of fabric, aware that Ket had popped out of the water a few feet away and was resting at the embankment edge.

Eron slid the clothing back on, then sat down with a frustrated sigh. He was really and truly alone out here right now. But he would never be spotted inside this cave. He'd have to take his chances out on the open water. He glanced around at the assorted piles of junk. He could probably build a raft, though it would not be a quick process to find pieces and make it sturdy enough to hold him. He wondered to himself if it might have been better if Ket hadn't saved him after all. At least drowning would have been a quicker death than dehydration in the middle of the ocean. He glanced over at the mer to see the gold eyes watching him, chin resting on folded arms, tail moving up and down thoughtfully. He couldn't be mad at Ket for saving his life, he supposed. At least he had a chance of survival now.

"I'm going to build a raft," he said, not sure if Ket understood that, but it seemed polite to at least let the mer know what he was planning to do, since he was going to use his collection. "Since I can't swim to land without my equipment."

Ket just watched him with wide eyes, and Eron sighed. It wasn't like he thought Ket might be helpful in building the raft, but it was disconcerting to have the mer watch him so closely all the time. He got up, took another swallow of the water that was running much lower than he had hoped, and then moved around to explore the cavern and its piles of stuff.

The amount was staggering, now that he had the time to really look. There were a variety of airship pieces, from canvas, to planks, to tools, to ballast weights. There were tools, clothing, and assorted items used by crews during the days they lived on the airship. He started to make a pile of stuff that might be useful, all the while feeling Ket's curious gaze on him. He found several more personal bags, most of which only held clothing. One of them had a package of crackers and dried meat, which he gratefully added to his food pile. There was a canteen inside it too, but the cap had come loose at some point, and there was no water inside of it. He tossed it aside with a frustrated sigh.

He became so lost in his search that he was not sure how long it had been, but when he looked up again, Ket was gone. Eron felt a bit of annoyance flutter in his chest. Ket was the reason he was here, he could have done something to help. Though what he expected the little fish creature to do anyway, he wasn't sure. He shoved a few bites of food into his mouth to keep his energy up before going back to work. He found a rusted hammer amongst the tools, but no nails or screws, so he was going to have to cobble something together with rope and wire.

The sun had started to sink, the cave half-filled with darkness, when he finally stopped his work. It was slow going, but he at least had the pieces set aside that he needed. He was sweaty and exhausted, and his body protested the hard work on a nearly-empty stomach. He ate another piece of dried meat and the rest of the cheese, saving a handful of fruit and nuts for the morning, along with the crackers and other jerky. He was in the middle of putting his clothes into one of the packs when a loud splash nearby caught his attention. He looked up to see Ket pulling himself up onto the stone ledge. He seemed more awkward than he usually was, because he had something looped across his body that he struggled to free. It was only after the petite mer had extracted himself from it that Eron saw it was the canteen he had discarded earlier. Ket set it down, then nudged it toward Eron with a shy glance through his lashes.

Eron frowned a little. "I can't drink sea water."

Ket stared at him, then nudged the canteen toward him again. Eron sighed and grabbed the strap to pull it to himself. He could at least use it to rinse off his sweaty face and hair. He opened the attached cap, then gave it a sniff, stopping short when he realized, it was not sea water after all. He blinked, turning his eyes to Ket, who watched him curiously in return. Eron hesitated a moment, then lifted it to his mouth to take a cautious sip. It was fresh water, cool and clean, the drops on his parched tongue the sweetest thing he had ever tasted. He took several large swallows before putting the cap securely back on and turning to Ket. "Where did you get fresh water?"

Ket gestured with one webbed hand toward the cave entrance, and the clicking sound filled the air again. Eron couldn't make any sense of it, but he realized that if Ket had brought him back fresh water within a day, land couldn't be too far away. That was an encouraging thought, at least. And Ket had done it without Eron saying a word about it to him, just seeing a need and an opportunity. He gave the mer a small, grateful smile. "Thank you," he said, holding up the canteen. "Thank you very much."

Ket's ear fins flickered eagerly, and he leaned in, much closer than he ever had before, and Eron jumped as the tip of the young mer's cool, wet nose pressed to his. It only lasted for a brief moment before Ket pulled back, ducking his head and gazing up at Eron shyly through his lashes again.

Eron felt something in the pit of his stomach. While he was not exactly sure what that meant, the nose touch had felt... intimate. Like he had been kissed. And the young mer was certainly acting like he had kissed him and was uncertain how Eron would feel about it. "Ket," he said softly, reaching up a hand, not sure what he was even trying to do. Ket blinked, then lifted one of his own webbed hands to meet his, and Eron pressed their palms and fingertips gently together. It was the most they had ever touched skin to skin, and it sent heat unexpectedly down his spine.

Ket gazed back at him, his ear fins lifting just a little. Eron hesitated a moment, then slowly leaned in. What was he doing? Ket wasn't human, they didn't even speak the same language, and yet, he felt something tugging inside of him, wanting the mer closer to him. Ket held still, his palm still pressed to Eron's. Eron paused for just a moment, then tipped his head to press his nose lightly against Ket's. Ket blinked and then pushed them together a little firmer. Eron reached up his hands to cup Ket's face in them, then shifted so his lips pressed to Ket's. The half-fish's lips were soft and surprisingly warm against his own, a little salty from the sea. Ket held still in Eron's touch until Eron pulled back, and then his ear fins fluttered just a little.

Eron sucked in a breath, letting his hands slowly slide down to hold Ket's bare shoulders. "Was that all right?" he asked, and Ket's ear fins gave a little shiver. Eron pointed to his own mouth, then to Ket's nose. "Kiss," he said.

Ket leaned in and pressed his mouth to Eron's. There was no suction or pressure behind it, just their lips touching, but Eron's heart gave an extra jump anyway. When Ket pulled back, ducking his head shyly again, Eron reached up to stroke a few damp strands of strawberry-blond hair behind Ket's ear fin, and the mer shivered.

"Kiss," Eron said again, then pointed to his own lips, puckering them for Ket to see.

Ket studied his mouth for a moment before his own lips formed into a strange little 'o' shape. He looked so much like a fish at that moment that Eron couldn't hold back a snort of laughter. "Almost," he said as Ket looked affronted. And then suddenly Ket had tackled him, knocking him backward onto the rocks, and pressed his nose to Eron's. Eron found himself with an armful of warm, damp skin and slick fish scales against his clothes, and he sucked in a breath as Ket's nose rubbed firmly against his. He leaned up to capture Ket's lips again, letting the mer cuddle on top of him. He slid his hands down Ket's surprisingly strong back, and the mer let out a sound like a squeak, blushing slightly. Eron chuckled at the new response, sitting up to cuddle Ket on his lap, the dark blue tail and fins resting on his legs. The mer tipped his face up and rubbed his head under Eron's chin like an oversized cat. "You're cute," Eron said, stroking his fingers through Ket's hair, which was surprisingly soft for being under the water most of the time. Ket let out a couple clicks in return.

Eron held him close for a moment, feeling his heart thudding in his chest and Ket's answering one in return. He had known Ket for only a short time, with only simple communication between them, but he was starting to feel something for the mer. Maybe that was from the shock of having nearly died, but he felt that there was something there, something beyond Ket saving a human from drowning when he hadn't had to.

He swallowed hard, looking down at the mer, who had snuggled into his arms contentedly. "Ket," he said, and Ket lifted his head. "You know I have to leave tomorrow, right?"

Ket gazed back at him, his fins moving at his temples in a motion that seemed almost sad. Eron swallowed. "Thank you again for saving me."

Ket gave him a shy smile and nestled close. Eron sighed and lowered Ket down onto the stones, moving over to his makeshift sleeping bag. He pulled the blanket over him, then lifted his head when he heard the shuffle of fins across the rocks. The mer was next to him, looking a little nervous. Eron stared back. "I'm going to sleep," he said. Ket's ear fins flicked in acknowledgement. Eron hesitated. "Did you... want to sleep next to me?"

Ket's ear fins moved again, his chin lifting hopefully. Eron swallowed. "Um, okay. Did you need a blanket or something?"

Ket's ear fins moved in what he thought was a 'no' gesture before Ket curled up next to him, his lithe body warm against Eron's even through the canvas. Eron cautiously draped an arm over him, not sure if that was appropriate or not, but Ket nestled into his embrace, letting out a silent, contented sigh. The mer's tail fin flicked gently against his leg in time with the lapping waves, and Eron fell asleep with Ket by his side on the cool rocks.

Chapter 4

WHEN HE WOKE UP the next morning, Eron could tell he was alone before he even opened his eyes. Ket had already become a familiar presence in their few days together, and when he was not there, the grotto seemed to be missing something. Eron thought maybe Ket had gone out hunting, but by the time the sun had fully risen in the sky and was heating the grotto, there was no sign of him. Eron was feeling more than a little nervous as he put the finishing touches on his raft. Had Ket truly gone and left him? He had seemed so attached to him, so eager for attention and praise. Had Eron's reminder that he had to leave been too much, and the mer didn't want to say goodbye?

The morning dragged on, with no sign of Ket. Eron moved back and forth to the entrance so many times, he lost count, but the young mer did not appear. If Ket was not back by the afternoon, he resolved he was going to have to take his chances on the sea with his makeshift raft. It was either that or potentially starve to death here. Neither was an appealing prospect, but indecision would kill him just as easily.

The sun had reached its peak overhead, the air as hot as an oven, and Eron was giving his raft a final balance test when there was a splash nearby. His head shot up, heart hammering in his chest, until his eyes met familiar amber ones. Ket slid up onto the little rock island, water sluicing off his skin and shimmering scales, and Eron felt unexpected relief at seeing him. And then Ket pulled something up onto the rocks, and Eron's breath caught in his throat.

It was his diving unit. Goggles, aircap, and air tank, all still fully intact. Ket slid the pieces up onto the rocks so they were sitting next to him, and Eron leaped the distance between the ledge and the rock outcropping to land next to Ket. He picked up the pieces, examining them carefully. Other than a few dents in the tank and one of the chains holding the goggles to the unit being broken, it looked completely whole and as usable as it had the day he had gone into the water with it.

He turned to Ket, who was watching him closely. "Did you go looking for this?" he asked, and Ket's ear fins fluttered. "For me?" The ear fins fluttered faster. "I..." Eron turned to look at the pieces at his feet, then back to Ket. "Thank you," he said, feeling like something was trapped in his throat and keeping him from swallowing. "Thank you so much." He leaned in and pressed his nose to Ket's. Ket looked a little surprised before he pulled back, dropping his eyes to the rocks.

The sadness in Ket's eyes sent a pain through Eron's chest that he was not expecting. Ket had gone to retrieve his dive gear, knowing that if he found it, Eron would definitely be leaving. And yet, he had done it anyway. "Ket," he started, but Ket suddenly grabbed something else that was tied to the diving gear with a piece of rope and pulled it up onto the rocks next to them. Eron knew it instantly. It was one of the emergency provision packs from the SERENITY's retrieval boat, with food and water for the crew, in case the airship was disabled and the crew needed to abandon it. He gasped, reaching for it reverently. He flipped open the top to find everything still sealed and protected from the sea water, only the outside of the pouch wet. He looked up Ket again, who was staring glumly at the rocks, looking for all the world like he was trying not to cry.

"Ket," he said, and the mer looked up. Eron gestured to the diving gear and the provisions. "Thank you," he said. "I don't know how to repay you for this. But thank you."

Ket glanced up at the mouth of the cave, then back to Eron. He made a few soft clicking and screeching sounds, motioning with his hand downward, then back up. "You... want me to stay until tomorrow?" Eron asked. Ket's ear fins flickered eagerly.

Something warm did a little dance in Eron's chest, but he just cleared his throat and shoved his hand through his dark hair. With the additional provisions, he was not going to starve before tomorrow, or even the day after. He could give Ket one more day, in gratitude for bringing him his diving equipment. "Um, yes, I can stay until tomorrow. I should check my gear anyway."

He almost tumbled into the water as Ket launched himself at Eron, wrapping his slender arms around him and burying his face in Eron's chest. He caught Ket against him as the mer's nose touched his, and then meshed their lips together in an ungraceful but enthusiastic kiss. Eron chuckled, then shifted as Ket's strong tail writhed against him eagerly, rubbing up against him in all the places it shouldn't. He tried to loosen Ket's grip around him, but the blond had suddenly become almost dead weight, cuddling closer still as his nose brushed over Eron's neck. Eron groaned. "Ket," he said, trying to formulate the words to make the mer stop before this got too out of hand, but Ket's nose brushed his collarbone, and then he felt the gentle nip of sharp teeth against his skin.

The brush of those teeth went straight to his cock, and Eron jumped. Ket pulled back, looking concerned for a moment, and Eron gave him a sheepish smile. "Sorry. You didn't hurt me."

Ket went back to nosing against him, nipping at Eron's neck and chest through his shirt, his heavy tail pressed firmly against Eron's groin. Eron tried to shift his legs to hide his growing erection. What the hell? Was he even considering fucking a half-fish creature? It wasn't like he couldn't get laid in Port Ceyran if he wanted to; but yet, Ket felt so nice in his arms. Soft and warm and smelling of salt air and sunshine. But he was leaving tomorrow, now that he had his dive gear back. He couldn't stay here, in this water-logged cave, for the rest of his life. Not that giving in to one night of... whatever this was meant he had to stay forever, but Eron didn't like the idea of a one-night stand, even with a non-human creature he had not known existed only days ago.

Ket continued to nose against his chest and stomach, which was doing nothing to help Eron's arousal. When he reached the bulge in Eron's pants, he looked up curiously. Eron flushed. "Uh..."

Ket tipped his head, then sat back onto one scaled hip. He gazed at Eron as his webbed fingers slid down his own stomach, over where the skin and scales combined. They slid further, past where human genitals would have been, until they were almost as low as human knees. Eron watched curiously, then blinked as Ket's fingertips suddenly parted a slit in the scales he had not noticed before. He could barely see the inside of it, but it looked pink and muscled, not entirely unlike human genitals. He felt heat flame on his face, and he cleared his throat. "Oh, I see... All right... Um, did you... want me to..." What did one call it if his partner was not human?

Ket reached up and took Eron's hand, drawing it down until it rested just above the opening. Eron chuckled nervously. "I guess that is a yes." He hesitated a moment, licking his lips, mouth suddenly gone very dry. Ket leaned up and pressed his nose to Eron's, holding it there for a moment before pulling back, giving him a sweet smile. Eron cleared his throat again. "Let me know if I do something wrong, okay?"

Ket gazed back at him, ear fins quivering a little. Eron slowly trailed his fingers down Ket's lower stomach, past where his groin would have been, then further until his fingertips hesitantly brushed the top of the slit on Ket's fin. The end of Ket's tail stirred a little, but otherwise, he did not move. Eron traced his finger over the length of the slit, from top to bottom. It was slick with a thick, clear liquid, and it felt warmer than the rest of the mer.

This has to be the strangest thing I have ever done, he thought to himself before he slowly pushed the first bit of one finger inside. It slid in easier than he had thought it would. Ket inhaled softly, his tail fin twitching a bit. "All right?" Eron asked, pausing the movement. Ket's ear fins quivered, and Eron pushed his finger further inside, moving slowly. The first few inches felt almost like a sponge, soft and flexible, but then, when his finger was over halfway in, the texture changed to firm muscle, more like what he was used to with human partners.

Once his finger was all the way in, Eron curled it a bit, exploring the tight passage. His finger found something inside like a rounded nub, and he stroked over it. Ket let out a slight hiss from the back of his throat. Eron started to pull back, thinking he might have hurt him, but Ket's muscles suddenly clamped down around the finger with surprising strength, keeping it in place. Eron gasped, and then Ket's nose touched his again. "Oh, you like that," he said and rubbed his finger over the spot again. Ket shuddered and clenched his muscles around him further.

Eron hesitated for just a moment, then carefully slid a second one inside next to the first, watching Ket for any signs of discomfort, but the mer's mouth was open in a silent gasp, eyes fluttering a little. He curled his fingers, finding the rounded spot again. He ran both fingers up the underside, and Ket threw back his head, letting out a silent cry of pleasure, his tail jerking a bit as his ear fins quivered. Pleased with that reaction, Eron did it again, and Ket clung tighter to him, mouth open in what looked like a yowl of pleasure, though no sound came out. Eron stroked over the spot, drawing his fingers back before pushing them in again and curling them. Ket squirmed underneath him, the end of his tail thumping gracelessly against the stone.

Eron felt the tight passage grow even tighter for a moment before something slid over his palm. He glanced down curiously. Rubbing over his hand, something stiff and pink and roughly phallic-shaped was protruding from the top of the slit where his fingers were still buried. It was only about as wide as his thumb and maybe as long as his middle finger, with no discernable head, covered with the same clear liquid that slicked the slit, and Eron realized that his fingers had been stroking the underside of it inside of Ket. "Oh," he said, staring down at it. "Is that good?" Ket's ear fins flickered. "Well, thank you," he said, reaching up his left hand to stroke over the shaft with his fingers. It looked rather delicate, but he realized it was stronger than it seemed, and he pinched his fingers around it, starting to stroke it slowly. Ket gasped and pushed his bottom half up higher eagerly.

This was going to take some practice, Eron realized as he tried to keep his right hand thrusting the fingers while stroking with his left, only one hand at a time wanting to really follow his commands with any sort of rhythm. He paused his left hand's movements as he wiggled his fingers inside of Ket's slick passage. The shaft glistened with the clear liquid, and he looked up at Ket. "Can I...?" He pointed to the shaft, then to his mouth. Ket blinked at him, as if not sure what he was asking. Eron had to wonder if maybe that was not a thing with the mer. "Stop me if it's not okay," he said before ducking his head down. He could smell the liquid as he got close, a little salty, a little sweet. He began to move his fingers again, making Ket squirm a little, before he opened his mouth and tentatively ran his tongue up the underside of Ket's shaft.

Ket shot up on his arms, his tail having gone rigid, his channel tightening almost painfully around Eron's fingers. Eron looked up in surprise. "Sorry, I can stop."

Ket blinked again, then slowly relaxed back down, gazing at him. For a moment, neither of them moved, until Ket pointed to his own mouth and then down at the slicked shaft, his ear fins giving a small, eager quiver. Eron laughed, feeling the tension leave him again. "Oh, you liked that, huh?" He leaned down and ran his tongue broadly up the taut underside. Ket threw back his head, his tail thumping eagerly as he writhed beneath him. Eron began to thrust his fingers in and out of the slit again as he closed his lips around the first inch of the thin... muscle? Organ? He wasn't really sure and decided that he didn't care. The liquid slicking it was nearly tasteless, just a hint of salt and sweetness. He sucked lightly on it, watching Ket jerk under him in apparent ecstasy. He wasn't a novice at blowjobs, but he was hardly doing anything at all, and Ket was already more enthusiastic and responsive than most of his previous partners.

It was easier to suck on the what-he-assumed-was-a-cock while keeping his fingers moving inside of Ket, so he did, sliding his mouth down further as his fingers continued to thrust. His tongue ran up the underside, and Ket let out a silent shriek of appreciation. Eron was slightly glad that Ket did not make any actual noise, because he was pretty sure he might have gone temporarily deaf if there had been a voice behind that cry. Ket's tail lashed back and forth, squirming and writhing and pushing his bottom half up toward Eron's lips, and Eron obliged by taking him as far into his mouth as he could, giving it a few strokes with his tongue. And then there was a gush of warm liquid over his hand from the slit, followed by a similar spurt from the cock in his mouth, and salty liquid hit the back of his throat. More than he would have expected, and Eron had to pull back, starting to cough, tears filling his eyes. He cleared his throat, swiping at his mouth with his sleeve.

Once he blinked the tears back, he glanced down to see Ket beneath him, completely boneless and limp, only the shallow rise and fall of his chest letting Eron know that he was even still alive. The shaft still protruded from the opening, and the clear fluid had coated most of Ket's scales beneath it, shimmering a little in the light. He watched Ket with concern, and then with fascination as the shaft slowly withdrew back inside of the slit, which then closed over until it was nearly hidden again in the scales and lines of Ket's tail. Other than that, the mer hadn't moved an inch. Eron frowned a moment. "Ket?"

The young mer's eyes had rolled back, but now they seemed to refocus on him, and Ket's tail gave a weak thump against the stone. Eron laughed, placing a hand lightly on a scaled hip. "That good?"

Ket's tail thumped appreciatively again, his ear fins giving a weak shiver too. Eron leaned down to brush a few strands of damp strawberry blond hair from Ket's eyes. "Are you all right?"

Ket's ear fins gave the acknowledging quiver, and Eron sat back. It wasn't like he knew anything about Ket's kind. Maybe this was a normal response? Either way, it certainly made him feel like he had done well; none of his other lays had ever almost passed out from his ministrations.

It was another minute or two before Ket pushed himself up on his arms, gazing at Eron through eyes that were still half-lidded and dazed-looking. Eron grinned. "Good?"

Ket's ear fins wiggled, and he shifted to nestle against Eron's chest. Eron couldn't stop a snort of laughter. "Oh, you're a snuggler, huh?"

Ket curled closer, and Eron kissed the top of his head. He pulled Ket close to him, then was suddenly reminded of his own raging erection that gave an eager buck between his legs against his trousers. He shifted uncomfortably, trying to will it to go away. He had pleasured Ket, and the mer still seemed a little out of himself; he was not going to push Ket away just to take care of his own need, even if he was so hard he could barely think straight.

After another minute, Ket opened his eyes, looking up at Eron, his tail fin giving an appreciative wave. He gave Eron's chest a light brush with his nose before he pulled away and slid into the water, flicking his tail around to clean the liquid off of it. Eron watched him, dipping his own slicked hand in the water. The water felt surprisingly cold now. Maybe a dip in it would help his aching cock. He pulled his shirt off, then loosened his pants, sighing with relief as his erection sprang free, the tip already leaking. He started to pull the pants off, then realized Ket was back on the rock, his golden-orange eyes focused on Eron's cock. "Oh, uh... It's all right," he said, not sure what he was reassuring Ket about. He pointed to his erection, then gestured to the area on Ket's tail. "Sort of like what you have going on... in... there."

Ket blinked, then almost jumped into Eron's arms again, grabbing his hand and sliding it down to brush over the slit on his tail. His nose pecked a kiss to Eron's cheek. "You want that again?" Ket's ear fins wiggled eagerly. Eron chuckled. "I think I've created a monster." Ket let out a huff and a series of clicking sounds that sounded like it might be chiding him. Eron leaned in to press their noses together. "All right, all right. Horny fish," he teased. Ket gave a roll of his eyes before shifting to lie back against the stone, the slit on his tail noticeably open and pulsing slightly.

The last few days had been the strangest of his life, and Eron was sure it was about to get stranger. But still, the ache between his legs persisted, his cock giving an eager, little jump. He could imagine if

Ket had been a human, he would be sprawled in a bed right now, legs spread invitingly, eager and dripping. That thought made his cock pulse again, and he ran his own fingers over it a moment, eliciting a groan from himself.

He swallowed hard, gazing at Ket. "It's all right if I...?" He motioned to his erection, then to the slit in Ket's tail. Ket's ear fins flickered, and his tail thumped, his eyes half-lidded in a way that made him look so ridiculously cute and wanton that Eron almost laughed. This was going to be weird, he thought as he slid up Ket's body, his knees on either side of Ket's tail. He brushed his fingers over the slit again, feeling it warm and slick beneath his touch, and Ket let out a breath of pleasure. Eron pressed a kiss to Ket's chest as he grabbed his own cock and positioned it at the slit before slowly pushing into him.

Ket tensed, and Eron stopped, the spongy insides of Ket's body clinging to him in a way that was both really odd and strangely sensual. "All right?"

Ket pressed his nose to Eron's and shifted a little under him before his ear fins flicked, and Eron slowly slid into him, Ket's warmth taking him deeper. He let out a moan, the sound amplified by the rocks around them. Ket squirmed beneath him, rocking his tail up until Eron was pushed all the way inside his tight passage. Eron let out a breath, already feeling sweat beading on his forehead and back from the tight heat and the humid air of the cave. He leaned down to press his nose to Ket's. "Okay?"

Ket clicked softly, his ear fins shivering, as his arms went up around Eron to pull him further down on top of him. Eron did his best to balance on the slick stones, not wanting to slip and crush Ket beneath him. His hips were pressed up against Ket's, feeling the warm, slightly rough scales against his skin. He stroked a hand through Ket's hair. Ket leaned into his touch, and Eron shivered as the mer's passage tightened around him. He slid his hips back, then forward again, starting up a slow rhythm. Ket let out a sound like a squeak that made Eron smirk in delight and kiss Ket again before the mer's mouth opened in a silent mewl. Eron rocked against Ket's, feeling the mer's tail thrash under him a little, and he began to work his hips faster. Ket writhed beneath him, his passage tightening rhythmically around Eron's length, making him gasp and moan loudly.

Something brushed against his cock, and Eron looked down to see that slender phallus protruding again from Ket's slit, rubbing up against his own length as he thrust. He slid his hand down to stroke over it as he jerked his hips harder into Ket, watching in fascinated delight as Ket yowled and jerked in near silent ecstasy. He wasn't going to last long with Ket moving against him like that, his body so tight and warm and slick, his cock sliding against Eron's own. He leaned down to kiss the mer's mouth eagerly, and his movements paused as Ket tightened around him, so tight he thought for a moment they might get stuck that way, before the mer unclenched and let him move again, feeling a rush through his head as he ground his hips against Ket's firmly. Ket clung to him with webbed fingers that dug lightly into Eron's sides as his tail shook and writhed beneath him. And then Ket clenched around him again, a gush of warm liquid flowing around his cock, and Eron couldn't hold back a shout as his own orgasm rocked through him, spilling himself into the mer's tight heat as a second rush of warm liquid from Ket's cock coated his stomach with a thick layer of sticky fluid.

Eron saw stars, and he almost lost his balance on the slippery stone, shifting just enough to land on his own arm rather than on top of Ket, feeling another warm rush go through his sensitive cock as he shifted, and Ket's passage tightened around him again. He carefully pulled out of the slit, rolling onto his side, still trying to catch his breath while Ket splayed limply next to him, the tip of his tail fins flicking the only movement. "Fuck," he groaned when he was able to formulate words again.

Ket let out a soft click that sounded like agreement, and Eron stroked his hand lightly over Ket's cheek. "You can say that again."

Ket's eyes opened, still hazy and floating, lying unmoving for another minute or two, and Eron let him rest there. Eventually, Ket shifted to curl into Eron's arms, tucking his head beneath the human's chin. Eron held him close, smelling the slight sweetness from Ket's pleasure against his own skin. "Doing all right?" Ket's ear fins fluttered against his skin, and Eron leaned down to press kisses into the strawberry blond hair. He fell asleep like that, Ket curved against his naked chest, the tip of Ket's tail draped over his leg, feeling the pulse of the mer's heart against his own in rhythm with the lapping waves.

Chapter 5

WAKING UP NEXT TO Ket was amazing. Waking up after sleeping naked on hard rock was not. Eron shifted, trying to find a comfortable position, but after a few minutes of tossing and turning, he gave up. Ket stirred next to him, yawning a wide yawn that showed off his conical teeth, stretching out as long as he could, before he rolled over into the water with a splash. Eron tried to stretch his own body out as Ket reappeared at the edge of the rocks. He pointed to the diving suit, then held up his hands in a motion that looked like it might be 'stop.' Eron frowned. "I do need to leave today, Ket," he said, keeping the words as gentle as he could.

Ket's ear fins twitched in agreement. He motioned to himself, then pointed to the entrance of the cave, then turned back to Eron and made the 'stop' gesture. Eron puzzled through that. "You need to go somewhere first, so I should stay here until you come back?"

Ket's ear fins twitched again, and Eron nodded. He still needed to eat and check his gear anyway. "All right," he agreed. "Just don't take too long. And be safe," he added, a little sternly. Ket blinked, then leaned up to press a quick kiss to Eron's mouth before he turned and dove under the water, vanishing in an instant.

Eron sighed as he washed himself off and dressed, then ate some of the provisions Ket had brought. Something inside of him ached as he realized he was going to be leaving. Last night had been fun, but more than that, there was something about Ket that drew him in, some part of him that wanted to protect the smaller mer and be there for him, the way that Ket had for him. That wasn't exactly practical with his job as a whall hunter either. His work was dangerous. And, from what he could tell, very few people knew about the mer; it wasn't like he could easily visit Ket while he was out hunting either. So this was probably going to be goodbye. And that hurt.

Eron had inspected his equipment and found it to be in good working order, despite the blows he had taken, when Ket suddenly reappeared, clicking eagerly at him. He gave Ket a weak smile. "Welcome back."

Ket swished his tail and motioned at Eron's diving gear. Eron blinked and held it up. "This?"

Ket's ear fins flicked. Eron held it out to Ket, who stared at it in confusion, then pointed at him. Eron let out a huff of laughter. "Oh, you want me to put it on?" Ket gave him a look that obviously meant yes, and Eron chuckled. "Sorry. I'm working on it."

He had put on his own sky diving clothes and had packed one of the water-resistant bags with all the food and water and a change of clothes. At the last moment he had added the journal with the drawing of the mer. Now he pulled on his diving suit with all of its straps and locks, making sure each one was secure, before he slid on the tank and its attached equipment. Ket watched the process curiously, and Eron gave him a small smile. "Not as simple for me to go swimming."

Ket's ear fins wiggled. Eron strapped the pack of supplies to his side, then hesitated. He swallowed hard and dropped to his knee on the stone. "Ket," he said softly, feeling the ache intensify inside of him.

Ket cocked his head to the side, then motioned eagerly with his hand for Eron to follow him. Eron blinked, watching as Ket dove into the water, and he didn't see him again until Ket's head popped up by the cave's entrance, waiting expectantly. "Are... you going with me?" he asked, and Ket rolled his eyes like he had asked a dumb question. Eron flushed, clearing his throat to cover his embarrassment. "All right." Something warm fluttered in his chest. This wasn't goodbye yet.

He secured his goggles over his eyes and put the aircap in his mouth. Down the channel, Ket looked like he was giggling at him. He ignored that, sliding into the water. Without his helmet, his clothing was going to get soaked again, but it was a price he was willing to pay. The coldness closed over his head, plunging him into sudden darkness, and he felt the familiar moment of not-quite-panic that he felt every time he went into the water. It only lasted for a second, and then he was swimming in the direction of the grotto entrance. He realized as he reached it that he couldn't see Ket, and his heart skipped a beat. Then the mer was beside him, and Eron stared in surprise. The way the light and shadow played over Ket's lustrous skin and tail made him nearly invisible in the murky water. Eron suddenly understood why the mer were not spotted often, even when the sky divers were under the water. Unless he knew what to look for, he might not have even noticed him.

Ket leaned in and pressed his nose to Eron's again before turning and motioning for Eron to follow him. The brief kiss made Eron feel hot all over, and Ket was nearly out of sight before he gave a kick and started after him. He realized with a momentary panic that Ket was extremely fast in the water, much more so than him even in his sleek whall hide diving suit, and he worried he would be left behind. But then Ket was back, giving him an apologetic look and slowing his movements so that Eron could follow him, the mer's tail just a few feet ahead of him. He gave Ket a grateful nod, determined to do his best not to slow the mer down too much.

The grotto was gone now, open water stretching before them. It was strange, seeing the ocean from this angle rather than above, and he wasn't sure that he liked it. His eyes darted around, watching for any movement in the murk, any flash of something that shouldn't be there. They were not very deep in the water, and it stretched beneath them, down into nothingness, where who knew what lived? They knew about whalls, and sharks, and tentacled creatures like giant squid and octopus. But they hadn't known about the mer. What else lay under the waves that humans didn't know about? A school of shiny, silver fish swam past him, and Eron nearly leaped out of his diving suit. Fuck, he was going to volunteer for deck duty on the airship for a while after this.

Ket swam a few paces ahead of him, and Eron admired how he cut through the water, his tail movements easy and elegant. Ket glanced back to see Eron watching, then did a few spins and acrobatic tumbles. Eron would have laughed if he had not been concentrating on keeping up with him. *What a showoff,* he mused, though it did not surprise him. Ket suddenly dove downward, and Eron lost sight of him.

Out of the darkness beneath him appeared a form, and Eron felt his heart pick up in his chest. It was a whall. One of the largest ones he had ever seen, and he had seen quite a few in his lifetime. He looked around in a panic for Ket. The young man was nowhere to be seen, and Eron stopped swimming, wondering if he was suddenly alone in this vast expanse of water.

Ket popped up beside him, skin gleaming in the light, holding still enough that Eron could make out all of the features on him. Ket gave him a grin and clicked a few times, then motioned downward. Eron stared at him with wide eyes behind his goggles. He couldn't be serious, wanting to go down there where the whall was; Ket was no bigger than one of the side fins on the large creature.

Ket suddenly dove again and vanished from Eron's view in that disconcerting way he did, and he inhaled sharply, looking around. The whall was almost directly below them, and he felt panic rise in his chest, the desire to swim to the surface itching beneath his skin.

And then Ket was next to him again, looking very annoyed, giving a few irritated-sounding clicks and a high-pitched squeaking noise that Eron hadn't heard before, motioning downward. Eron shook his head, pointing to the whall that lazily swam below them. Ket let out a huff, and then he had caught Eron's arm and dove straight down, taking Eron with him at a speed that made his stomach rise in his throat. He tried to resist, but Ket's momentum was too strong, and he clapped his hand to his aircap and goggles to keep them in place as he was unwillingly dragged downward into the dark depths of the sea.

They leveled out, and Eron pulled his hand away from his goggles to see that they were swimming right next to the whall. Its eye was nearly all black with a large, round pupil, and it seemed to be looking right at Eron. He tried to jerk backward, but Ket still had a hold on his arm, drawing him along by his side as they swam.

Ket let out a series of clicks and screeching sounds, and the whall made a low, rumbling noise back, the vibrations of it going through Eron like the beat of a drum. He watched in terror as Ket reached out and ran one of his hands over the side of the whall's face between its eye and the corner of its large mouth. The whall made another sound, higher this time. Ket then yanked him forward and pressed Eron's hand against the whall, his own face mere inches from the whall's staring eye. He tried to pull back, but Ket held him firmly in place, gazing expectantly at him. When he didn't move, Ket moved their hands so his palm stroked over the whall's skin. It was slick and a little rough, but he could feel the power behind it. Power he had speared many times over. He knew what that power could do. He was here because of it. He tried to pull his hand back again, but Ket held it firmly in place with surprising strength for his small frame, giving Eron a pointed look.

Eron swallowed hard. The whall could open its mouth and easily swallow both him and Ket whole. But yet the creature here just blinked at him. It was obvious that Ket had done this many times before. Eron glanced over at Ket, who gave him an encouraging smile, and Eron slowly ran his hand over the whall's cheek, the way Ket had done. The whall did not move, but next to him, Ket looked extremely pleased.

Ket gave his hand a tug and swam down under the whall, reaching up to skim his fingers over its belly as they did, coming up on its other side. That was when Eron had the biggest surprise of all. Only a few feet away, swimming alongside the whall, barely visible in the dark water, was a group of around a dozen mer just like Ket. They all had tail fins in various hues of blue and green, and their skin had the same sort of shimmery iridescence, though their hair was a variety of colors and lengths.

Ket still held his hand and moved closer to the group, making a bright chittering noise that Eron assumed was a greeting. A few of the mer chattered back. One of them, with the same beautiful but androgynous sort of look that Ket had, swam over to touch noses with Ket, and Eron felt an unexpected stab of jealousy as Ket seemed to giggle and touch noses in return.

Two of the mer were holding something between them as they swam, and when the light caught them just right, Eron was able to see that it was a smaller mer, with a bigger head and eyes, tail fin swishing awkwardly behind it in an unsteady rhythm. The other two held its chubby arms, and Eron realized with a start that he was looking at a child mer, probably not any older than his own toddler niece. He stared at the child for a moment in fascination, then almost leaped out of his skin when a shape suddenly moved in between him and the trio. He looked up a heavily muscled chest into the face of another mer, with long, black hair that swirled around his shoulders and dark eyes that were glowering at him. The new mer studied him closely for a moment, and Eron felt Ket's grip on his hand tighten just a little.

Then the bigger mer turned to Ket and said something to him in their clicking language, and Ket sidled a bit closer to Eron as he replied. Without understanding a word of what they were saying, Eron was sure that this other mer had once been or tried to be romantically involved with Ket. He had seen enough fights and arguments between exes break out in various bars or on street corners that he recognized the way Ket turned aside just a little. That sent another hot spike of jealousy through his body, and he pulled Ket closer to his side, feeling the smaller mer shift against him.

The dark-haired mer looked Eron up and down, and Eron straightened up to his full height, trying to look intimidating, as much as he could in a diving suit under the water, though he wasn't sure he was very successful. The other mer was larger than him, and without his aircap and tank, he would have no ability to do anything underwater. Ket exchanged a few more sounds with the dark-haired mer, who finally gave Eron a glower and a swish of his tail that nearly knocked his goggles off Eron's face as he retreated. Ket gave Eron's arm an apologetic snuggle before drawing him along with the group of mer swimming next to the whall.

Eron was feeling more and more like a fish out of water as Ket pulled him along with the... school? Pod? Herd? Whatever it was, the group of mer all watched him with varying levels of curiosity and animosity, though none with as much revulsion as the dark-haired mer, who looked like he wanted to snatch Ket from Eron's arms. He also felt awkward as hell. He had no idea where they were going, literally being dragged along by the petite blond. They had to be going somewhere, right? Ket knew that he couldn't just swim under the water indefinitely with them. He was also starting to get tired. His several days of only emergency rations was catching up to him, and he was going to have to take a break and eat soon, though preferably not in the middle of the sea.

Next to them, the whall made a sound, and Ket slowed, as did the rest of the mer. Eron watched as the whall drifted toward the surface. He glanced uneasily around, suddenly felt very exposed in the nothingness without the large whall right next to them. The two mer with the little one surrounded it with their fins protectively, their eyes flicking nervously about. All of the mer drew closer together into a tight circle, scanning the area around them, just as he was.

The whall was at the surface for several minutes, expelling the ocean byproducts through the blowhole on its head before it dove again to rejoin the group of mer. Eron felt the tension in Ket release as the whall settled back into its place, the mer parents going back to helping the little one swim along with them. Eron felt a stab of ice in his stomach as realization dawned. The whall was acting as protection for the mer. Besides their teeth and their camouflage ability, the mer had no defense against things that could hurt them; they were as vulnerable to ocean predators as humans might be to bears or wild cats. He had seen several dangerous creatures with his own eyes over the years. And those were just things he knew about. The ocean was vast and so deep that the bottom could not be reached in many places; who knew what other types of terrors might lurk there that could do harm to the mer with their soft skin and minimal defense? Their camouflage would only work so well when dealing with a larger predator. But whalls were plant-eaters. They were also the largest creatures in the seas (*that we know of,* he reminded himself,) so their size and strength alone could potentially deter an attack from other ocean-dwelling monsters.

But not humans. Whalls had no natural predators in the ocean. But they did in the air.

Understanding hit him and made him dizzy. He had spent seven years killing whalls. Dozens of whalls. Maybe hundreds, he didn't even know. Did every group of mer have a whall for protection that he had wiped out for something as simple as profit? Eron felt his hands start to tremble. He wanted to throw up and scream and cry all at once, but he could do none of those things in the water. He reached out, his fingers brushing over Ket's tail, and Ket looked back with so much concern that Eron almost lost his composure anyway, his goggles steaming up with hot tears behind the lenses. Ket motioned upward, seeming to ask him if he needed a break, but Eron realized as he glanced around that this was not the time for him to stop the group for his own revelations, no matter how devastating. He could break down later, sometime when it was just him and Ket. He had had to soldier on through painful moments before in his whalling career; he could do it again now.

It felt like they had been swimming for hours when Eron finally was flagging too much to continue. Ket gave him a concerned look, then said something to the whall and the other mer, and they all circled while the whall went up to the surface, Ket and Eron following. Eron worried that he might not have anywhere to rest, but there was a large, flat plank of wood, maybe the top of a box create, floating nearby, and it was sturdy enough to hold his weight as he climbed onto it. Ket bobbed in the water next to him, the whall a short distance away. Eron immediately pulled off his goggles and searched the air for any sky diver ships, but the sky was darkening with storm clouds. Most airships would have either landed on the water or returned to port when bad weather was imminent. He was thankful for that small blessing as he pulled the water and food from his pouch, taking a long drink. He nibbled at a piece of dried meat, offering a bite to Ket, who took it and ate it in his awkward chewing way that made Eron smile.

A loud noise startled him. It was the whall blowing out the sea waste through its blowhole. He realized he had never heard it that close before. He watched it for a moment, then turned to Ket, his eyes downcast. "Do... do the whalls protect you?"

Ket blinked at him, then nodded solemnly. Eron groaned as his fear was confirmed. "Ket, you know that I hunt whalls for a living, right?"

Ket gazed back at him, his eyes full of something that looked very much like sadness, but his ear fins wiggled in their 'yes' motion. Eron shoved another bite in his mouth so he didn't have to say anything for a minute before slowly responding, "What happens if the whall protecting you gets attacked by... by people like me?"

Ket frowned a moment, then pressed his hands together before spreading his arms wide. "You scatter?" Eron guessed, and Ket's ear fins wiggled. Eron felt his stomach drop inside of him. A single mer or two alone in the water would be easy prey for other creatures, or even humans, if humans knew about them. He thought about the little child mer in their group. Most of the mer looked to be adults.

Ket was one of the youngest-looking ones, and he still didn't look like a child. How many mer could there be in the ocean if so few people knew about them? Wouldn't there be more children too? What had happened to all of them?

A terrible thought occurred to him. "Wait... Were you out there all alone finding me food and my diving gear?"

Ket looked embarrassed but wiggled his ear fins in acknowledgement. Eron scowled. "Ket. You shouldn't have done that."

Ket's golden-orange eyes narrowed at him, and he gave Eron several irritated-sounding clicks and screeches that he was sure was a rebuttal that Eron had human needs that needed tending to. "You could have died out there," Eron scolded. "You risked enough trying to save me the first time."

Ket glowered at him, crossing his arms over his chest pointedly. Eron frowned. "Just promise me you won't do anything like that again, all right?"

Ket wrinkled his nose, then gave a sudden flip of his tail that flung water droplets at Eron, making him jump and nearly capsize his makeshift raft. "Hey!" he said, giving Ket another glare. "I mean it. I don't want you getting hurt. Especially not because of me." And that was the truth, he realized. Ket had risked his life several times over, saving Eron from the shipwreck, bringing him supplies, finding his lost equipment, and contacting his group of mer to escort them. If the sweet, young mer had been injured or killed, it would have been Eron's fault, and that made his heart leap into his throat.

Ket huffed and looked more than a little sulky, but he wriggled his ear fins in ascent. Eron hesitated, then shifted a little to lean down and press his nose to Ket's, nearly falling off the wood, but he didn't care. The delight in Ket's eyes when he did it sent warmth through his whole body. Then Ket's arms were around his neck, their lips pressed together in a sloppy but eager kiss. Eron pulled Ket up out of the water with surprising ease, and the mer nestled onto his lap and kissed him again.

He swallowed hard, cuddling Ket close despite both of them being quite soggy. A drop of water hit his upper cheek, and he thought for a second that it came from Ket, but then another hit the top of his head, and fat raindrops began to fall around them.

A sharp click sounded nearby, and Eron turned to see the dark-haired mer poking his head out of the water, giving both of them a slight glare, his ear fins flicking in a way that Eron could tell meant he was annoyed at finding them like that. Ket let out another huff but detached himself from Eron. He pointed at the sky, then motioned that they should get back in the water. Eron couldn't disagree with that as a low rumble of thunder sounded. He pulled on his goggles, adjusted his aircap, and then followed Ket back into the sea.

Chapter 6

WHEN THEY CAME UP to the surface again what must have been a few hours later, Eron almost danced for joy. Land was nearby. It was not the mainland of Port Ceyran, that much he could tell. This looked like it might be an island. He could see a smudge of shadow on the horizon that he thought might be the mainland, but it was already growing dark, and it was darker still with the storm clouds and the light rain still falling. There was no way in his exhausted state he would be able to make it to that distant shore before darkness turned the sky and the sea the same color. But, he realized as he looked at the island, there was a settlement there. A small town, with one very large, grand house around it. He could see several airships docked, some on water, some on land. One of them looked almost exactly like the SERENITY. A whalling ship. His stomach surged, and he searched the sky for any sign of an airship that could be hunting their own whall right now, but the sky was still clear of vessels.

Ket gave his arm a tug, his ear fins flickering eagerly, and Eron realized with relief that Ket had purposefully brought him to this inhabited island. With a town, his own ship could be contacted to let them know he was all right, and the airships of the island could transport him back to the mainland. He pulled the aircap from his mouth so he could talk to Ket. "Thank you," he said, gesturing at the island.

Ket clicked a few times, then leaned in, pressing his nose to Eron's. Eron pressed back gently, but when Ket pulled away, the young mer's face had fallen. Eron frowned, reaching up to touch Ket's cheek. "Do you have to go?"

Ket blinked, then hesitantly moved his ears in a 'no' gesture. Eron inhaled sharply, his heart giving a small surge in his chest. "I'm not ready to leave you if you don't have to leave me," he said. Ket's ear fins flickered hopefully, his face lighting up, and Eron gave him another nose press before pulling back. "Will your friends be all right without you?" Ket's ear fins wriggled. Eron grinned. "Come on, then, silly fish, let's find some place we can both rest."

Ket flicked his ear fins, then dove down beneath the water. Eron ducked his head so he could watch Ket below him, clicking and chattering at the other mer as his hand brushed over the whall's cheek again. There was a short conversation exchanged between Ket and several of the mer. The dark-haired one moved forward like he might try to grab Ket's arm, but Ket let out a sound that even in the water sounded like a hiss, and the dark-haired mer backed off, giving Eron a glower. Eron found himself glad he had not been found by that mer when their retrieval boat had capsized; he had a feeling that one would have taken great delight in seeing him drown.

Ket gave another chirp and patted the whall's side, and then he swam up to Eron, inclining his head for Eron to follow. Eron hesitantly held up his hand at the mer in what he hoped was a friendly, grateful gesture, before following quickly after Ket, not wanting to be too far behind. He kept an eye out for any sign of danger, though he suspected that this close to the surface the most dangerous thing they could encounter would be other humans. He wondered if anyone might spot Ket in the water, though his dark fins and the light playing across his skin still seemed like decent camouflage with the tossing surf above them.

They were drawing closer to the island. Ket seemed to be looking for something, though Eron didn't know what. The water was growing shallower, and he hoped that Ket was not going to just land them on the beach in plain sight of anyone nearby. But he realized he shouldn't have worried; the mer seemed to be quite good at hiding from humans, and Ket was no exception. Ket swam through a narrow crag and then into a small area inside a rock cliff where the water made a little bay, similar to the grotto they had come from. There was a large stretch of rock and sand, and far in the distance, Eron could see a bit of light. This tunnel seemed to go straight through the cliff from the sea to the land.

It was fairly dark where they were, but Eron crawled up on the shore and laid there gratefully. All of his muscles hurt; that was more swimming in one day than he had done most of his life. He was envious of Ket's sleek ability to shoot through the water in a way that he never would be able to imitate. He pulled his goggles off and rested on the sand for a while, breathing in the briny air of the cave. He felt a bump on his arm, and he turned to see Ket nudging him worriedly. He gave him a weak smile. "I'm fine. Just tired. I'm not used to swimming all day like you."

Ket beamed and curled up next to him, snuggling close. Eron held him tight, Ket's damp skin warm in his arms. He was going to miss this. "Are you hungry?" he asked after a moment, his stomach rumbling against the mer. Ket smiled at him, then motioned to the water. Eron let go of him, and Ket slid down until he plunged under the surface, disappearing from view. Eron took the time to remove his air tank and his sodden clothes, replacing them with the fresh ones in his pack and pulling out some of his water and provisions.

He was just draping his wet clothes over a few rocks to let them dry when Ket reappeared, a fish clamped tightly in his teeth. Relief that Eron had not been expecting flooded him when Ket slid onto the rocks and deposited his catch there. "Welcome back."

Ket clicked a few times before motioning for Eron to sit next to him. He picked up the fish and bit into it with his sharp teeth as Eron dug into his own provisions. They ate in contented silence for a few minutes, the only sound the lap of the waves on the shore nearby. Eron offered Ket bites of his own food, and Ket tried some of the nuts and dried fruit. The nuts seemed to confuse him, and the dried fruit looked even more awkward for him to chew than the dried meat, until Ket discovered he could swallow the fruit whole. He smacked his lips and clicked eagerly at Eron, and Eron felt warmth spread through him. Fresh fruit would probably taste even better to the mer. Perhaps he could find some and bring it back to him, if Ket stayed nearby. Which brought him around to the moment he had been dreading the last few days.

"Ket," he said, and Ket paused with his teeth sunk into a bite of fish. Eron made a face and waved at him to continue eating before he said, "I really appreciate you saving me and helping me to land. You didn't have to, but you did, and I... I'm really grateful. Thank you."

Ket beamed at him, his ear fins wiggling. Eron swallowed hard. Time to address the issue. "I'm not sure how you feel, but I... I really like you. And not just because you saved me."

Ket stared at him for a moment before he slowly held out one webbed hand, and Eron took it, feeling his chest clench. "I don't want to leave you all alone," he said, licking his lips as he tried to formulate his racing thoughts into coherent words. "But I'm a whall hunter." Ket looked sadly at him, and Eron shook his head quickly. "I mean, I *was* a whall hunter. I promise you I'm done with that when I get back to the mainland."

Ket beamed, and Eron suddenly found himself with an armful of wiggly mer. Ket's lips pressed to Eron's, and he kissed him before pushing him back, wiping at his mouth. "Maybe don't kiss me with fish breath. I know mine's not much better, but that's pretty bad."

Ket stuck out his tongue at him, and Eron choked on a laugh before he sobered again. "My point is... I'm human, and you're... you're not. I can't live in the water with you, and I'm pretty sure you can't live on land with me."

Ket frowned thoughtfully at that, then waved his hand vaguely, but his eyes had gone very sad. Eron exhaled a breath. "I don't know what to do. If I'm going to be in the water, it would be as a whall hunter, and I don't want to put you, or any of your friends, in danger. Especially since the world doesn't know about you yet."

Ket's ear fins flicked a little and pointed backward, making him look so sad that Eron was almost brought to tears himself. "Would you want me to stay with you if I could?"

Ket's ear fins wiggled eagerly. Eron sighed and pulled the mer close, giving him a warm hug. "All right. I'm not going anywhere tonight. Let me think."

Ket brightened a little at that, curling into his arms. Eron stroked Ket's hair, which seemed to soothe both of them. He was exhausted, but he didn't want to let go of the mer, so he scooped him up in his arms and moved over to a softer patch of dry ground. Ket spooned back against him, and Eron fell asleep with his hand resting on Ket's scaly hip.

It was still dark out when Eron woke up, Ket burrowed into his arms. He didn't want to move, but his muscles were crying out to stretch. He carefully extricated himself from around Ket, who slept on, and he took a few steps away so he could flex and move his body until some of the soreness had abated. Then he opened his pack and pulled out some food and water, nibbling at them as he tried to think. He didn't want to leave Ket. Not yet. But what could he do? Even if Ket could survive on land, he couldn't just put him over his shoulder like a blanket and carry him around, though that thought did make him smile to himself. Where could he possibly go so he might be able to see the mer again? He wasn't bound to his terrible apartment in Port Ceyran; in all honesty, he was hardly ever there with most of his time spent on airships. He had a decent amount of money saved. Perhaps he could buy a small houseship of his own, which was doable with only himself, but not cheap. But then what? He was only twenty-seven, and even if he was frugal, he would eventually need another job to keep up with repairs and other expenses.

A rustling nearby drew his attention, and he turned to see Ket stretching lazily on the sand. The sunlight was starting to come into the cave, and it danced over Ket's blue scales, making them shimmer like the ocean from above. He watched the mer stretch and yawn, that long, powerful tail flicking lazily. Then Ket rolled over and saw him, his golden eyes lighting up. He let out a cheerful clicking sound that warmed Eron down to his toes. "Good morning to you too. Sleep well?"

Ket let out a squeak, brushing sand out of his hair. Eron sighed and gave another stretch himself. "I don't know how you can swim all day. I'm fucking sore!"

Ket let out a sound that might have been a giggle, wiggling his fin playfully at Eron. "Yeah, yeah, you're built for it," Eron agreed. He gave Ket a smile, which slowly faded away. "Can we talk?"

Ket immediately looked sad, hanging his head a little, but he shifted to sit facing Eron, ear fins perked up to listen.

Eron sighed. "I... I can't thank you enough for everything you've done for me," he said softly. "You've saved my life so many times in the last few days, and you didn't have to do any of it."

Ket looked up at him and smiled shyly. He looked so hopeful that Eron had to look away to keep his throat from constricting so he couldn't talk. "I know we don't exactly speak the same language, so I can't know exactly what you're thinking or what you want, but..." He looked up to meet Ket's round eyes with his own gray ones. "I know that I like you, and... if I have to leave you forever, I'd be sad."

Ket's eyes narrowed, and he looked like he might cry. Eron quickly crawled over to him and wrapped his arms around the mer, who cuddled into his embrace. "That would make you sad too?"

He felt Ket's ear fins flutter against his neck, which sent a shiver down his spine. "I barely know anything about you or your kind. But I'd like to learn what I can." He stroked a hand down Ket's back, feeling the mer squirm a little in his lap, and a worrisome thought suddenly occurred to him. "Um... you're not... pregnant, or mated for life to me, or anything, are you?"

Ket pulled back in surprise, blinking at him before giving a small smile and shaking his head, his ear fins flickering 'no.' Eron let out a breath. "Okay, just checking. Sorry if that was weird."

Ket clicked a soft laugh and curled into his arms again. Eron held him for another moment. He had had a few relationships before, but nothing really long-term. As a sky diver, he was gone so often, and his life was so uncertain, it hadn't seemed fair to do that to anyone. But this felt different than anything he had experienced before. It was strange and probably more than a little absurd, but he could deal with those feelings. "If I could find a way to stay with you, would that be something you'd want?" Ket's nose pressed up to his, and Eron stroked a hand over his hair. "Okay. I'm still not sure what the answer is, but I will not leave without telling you. I promise that."

Ket gave him a weak smile, his tail giving a small flip that Eron sensed was him trying to show any enthusiasm right now. "I will come back right here to this spot before it gets completely dark tonight, all right? I swear it."

Ket's arms went around Eron's neck tightly. Eron hugged him close. "Will you be safe until then?"

Ket let out a click that Eron had come to understand meant 'yes', and he pulled back to stroke a hand down Ket's cheek. "I will be back. Just stay out of sight and out of danger, all right?"

Ket's ear fins flicked. Eron leaned in and kissed him again for a long moment before he reluctantly let go of Ket and rose to his feet. Ket slumped on the rocks, looking dejected, and if he had not had a moment of dizziness from his rationing of water, Eron might have stayed. He picked up his gear, then turned to Ket again, who had not moved. "I'll see you tonight, silly fish," he said, and Ket gave an ear fin wriggle. Eron turned and started toward the light at the far end of the cave, feeling Ket's eyes on him with each crunch of his boots on the rocky ground. He forced himself to keep walking even as each step made him feel heavier and heavier. The opening was growing larger and brighter until he was only a few steps from the early morning sunlight that streamed in. He chanced a glance back over his shoulder. Ket was still where he had left him on the rock at the edge of the water, so small in the distance, but he was there. Eron reached out toward him and then pressed his hand to his chest. He saw Ket's tail fin raise and wave back at him like a flag in the wind, and he smiled before he took a deep breath, turned, and stepped out into the brilliant sunlight.

Once his eyes adjusted, Eron saw that outside the cave appeared to be a stretch of sandy beach, but he could see a slightly overgrown path not too far away that led up to the dwellings. He headed for it, glancing around as he walked to see if he could figure out where he was. He could see the infrastructure for steam power and desalination, so the island had fresh water. He counted four airships of various sizes anchored to the ground, one of which was specifically a whall hunting vessel, and he suppressed a shudder.

The house that seemed to be at the top of the hill in the center of the island was large and very grand; he could tell that without even being close to it. The smaller houses around it were clean and habitable, but they were not ostentatious. Eron had no idea who might live in the large, grand house, but at the moment, he was more concerned with finding food and water and a way to contact his whalling team. He wondered how they would react to him being alive and what they would think of Ket. Then he thought maybe it wouldn't be a good idea to tell them about Ket for a while. But maybe he'd want to tell them if he tried to explain why hunting whalls was something he was no longer willing to do. They were his friends, his team. But they also hunted to make a living. This whole line of thought was giving him a headache.

He reached the edge of the little town, already seeing a few window shades open. He was glancing around to try to figure out which door to knock on when one to his left opened, and a woman stepped out. Her brown hair was streaked with gray and up in a bun. She was not very tall, even with the heeled boots she wore. She had on form-fitting black pants and a white blouse, and over that she wore a one-piece brown and gray striped jacket with long sleeves, a corseted top, and long coat tails, the front panel open to show a short, white ruffled skirt over it. It looked to Eron like some kind of uniform, as there were very few embellishments on it. She was pulling on a pair of fingerless gloves, but when Eron moved, she looked up in surprise. Her eyes were light brown, her face lined with tension more than age.

Eron quickly raised his hand in greeting. "Hi. I'm sorry if I startled you."

The woman glanced up and down at him, and Eron suddenly felt very underdressed without at least a waistcoat to make himself more presentable. He shifted his diving equipment so she could see it better. "My name is Eron. Eron Marcel. I was part of a whalling crew that was shipwrecked a few days ago, I just made it back to land."

"Oh!" the woman exclaimed, suddenly seeming much more at ease with his casual appearance. "I'm so sorry to hear that. I mean, I'm glad you're alive. But I'm sorry to hear that you were in a shipwreck. Are you all right? Are you hurt?"

Eron wasn't quite sure what to reply to first, so he said, "I'm doing all right. I've had limited food and water for a while though."

The woman frowned, but it was obviously directed at his situation and not at him. "I can only imagine! You poor thing. Marcus!" she called, turning toward the open doorway.

After a moment, a man of similar age appeared in the doorway in an outfit that looked to Eron like the male equivalent of the woman's uniform. The graying fuzz of his dark hair stood out from his sepia-toned skin as he stared at Eron.

The woman turned to Marcus. "This poor young man has washed up from a shipwreck. Will you please tell Lettie I'll be in a little later once I get him some food and fresh clothes?"

Marcus nodded, then leaned down to ask her something that Eron could not hear, but he suspected it was something about if she would be fine alone in the house with a strange man. The woman laughed and gave him a light nudge in the ribs. "It's all right, dear, don't worry about me. I'll bring him with me up to the big house shortly."

Marcus glanced over at Eron again, then gave the woman a kiss. "All right, Mae. I'll see you shortly." He gave Eron a stern look. Marcus was not any taller than Eron, but he was much broader, and his face had several hardened lines pressed into it that spoke of a world-weariness that Eron recognized all too well from the city. He knew that if they were to get into a fight, Marcus would likely come out the victor. "No funny business, son."

"Absolutely none, sir," Eron tried to reassure him.

Marcus moved past Eron to the walking path that led toward the house on the hill. Once he was on his way, the woman motioned with her head for Eron to follow her inside the small house. Eron immediately felt his mouth water as he smelled the remnants of a breakfast that must have been bacon and some sort of fried cake. The woman motioned to a chair at a small kitchen table. "Sit. I'll get you some food. I think the kettle is still warm." Eron felt his heart lurch just a little at the word as she picked up the copper tea kettle from the stovetop. "Mr. Marcel, was it?"

"Yes, ma'am, but please, call me Eron," Eron said, setting his things by the door and toeing off his dirty boots before moving to sit in the indicated chair.

The woman chuckled and gave him a warm smile that reminded Eron more than a little of his own mother. "All right. Eron then. I'm Maeve. Maeve Wilder-Smith. You can call me Maeve. That was my husband, Marcus." She set down a cup of steaming tea in front of him. "If you're all right waiting, I can make you some bacon and eggs."

"I would really appreciate it," Eron said, giving her a grateful smile. "But please don't put yourself out too much. And I'll be glad to pay for the trouble."

Maeve waved her hand airily as she set to bustling around the kitchen. "No need, no need, but you're such a sweetie to offer. No, I have a son probably close to your age. How old are you, dear, twenty-five?"

"Twenty-seven," Eron replied, and Maeve let out a giggle.

"My Nelson is twenty-four. He works in a factory in Port Ceyran. Makes pieces for airships and steam engines. It's a thankless task, but someone has to do it. Of course, everyone would notice as soon as production stopped. Always those on the bottom who aren't appreciated until they are gone, isn't that right? I'd certainly hope that if my boy were in need, some nice person would give him a helping hand. I think every mother sees a little bit of her son in each young man. Does your own mother know you're all right, dear? Do we need to send a message to the port? Oh! Forgive me! I don't even know if your family is alive or if you are close with them. I'm sorry. It's been so long since we've had someone new here, my head is just running away with me."

Eron was finding it easy to like Maeve, and the toasted bread and bacon she was making didn't hurt either. "My mother is alive. And my father. But they don't live in Port Ceyran. My sister does though, with her husband and my niece."

"Oh, that's nice," Maeve said with another beaming smile. "Well, we'll get some food in you and get you cleaned up, and then we'll go to the big house and send a message to her to let her know you're all right."

"The big house?" Eron questioned, picking up his tea and giving it a careful sip. It was deliciously warm, if not a bit bland, but he did not care, swallowing another mouthful that sent warmth all the way down to his toes.

"Yes. I suppose you have no idea where you are, silly me," Maeve said, waving her spatula enthusiastically. "This is actually a private island. It's owned by Baron Forthwell. Thaddeus Forthwell, maybe you've heard of him? Oh, you said you were on a whalling crew. I would bet that he is the owner of your airship. He owns just about every whalling company that's out there, it seems." Maeve took a breath, rubbing her finger thoughtfully over her lips.

The name was only vaguely familiar to him, as if he had maybe read it in the newspaper once or twice. But if this Thaddeus Forthwell owned a fleet of whalling ships, Eron was sure he would be quite rich, with how much whall oil was prized. Of course, that meant that any whall in the area would be in danger. He made a mental note to tell Ket to let the mer and the whalls know to stay away from this island. "So he owns the big house up the hill?"

"Yes," Maeve said, giving the toast a dramatic flip. "Everyone on this island works for him in some capacity. Cleaning, cooking, his own airship crew, that sort of thing. He goes to the mainland several times a week, of course, but he just arrived home yesterday, right before that nasty storm hit, so he will be here today. And even if he wasn't, his-" Maeve cut herself off so suddenly that Eron had to look up to make sure she was all right. Maeve gave him an apologetic look. "Sorry. His daughter would probably be here if he was not."

From the way that last line came out, Eron was sure that Maeve was not fond of Baron Forthwell's daughter. "How old is his daughter?"

"Oh, goodness, she must be… early thirties?" Maeve said thoughtfully. "Older than you, but younger than me. Heavens, I'm closer to the baron's age, of course. Her name is Lyla. She's a… a doctor, I guess you could say? A scientist? An inventor?" Maeve sounded like she was asking Eron, as if he knew the answer. "Well, I'm not sure exactly what her specialty is, but she works for her father. You'd be wise to steer clear of her, dear."

"Why?" Eron asked, taking another sip of his tea.

"She's… odd," Maeve said, in a tone that Eron could tell meant she was trying to not say something impolite. "She and her father are similar, but where his mind is about business, hers is about technology, and sometimes she gets a little carried away." Maeve pursed her lips as she pulled a plate from a cupboard and scooped up the food onto it. "Here you are, dear, I'll get you some more tea."

She placed it down in front of him, and Eron almost melted with delight. Crisp strips of bacon, and a piece of buttered toast with a fried egg over the top. His own mother used to make him breakfast like this when he was younger. He figured Maeve and Marcus had to be around his own parents' age.

Maeve poured more tea into his almost empty cup. "There now. You eat, I'm going to go draw you a bath and find something more appropriate for you to wear."

"Thank you," Eron said, sure that he smelled more than a little ripe after the days of exertion and no clean water for bathing. Maeve gave him another bright smile before vanishing down the hall. Eron dug into the meal, almost moaning in delight at the delicious flavor. He vaguely wondered if Ket would like bacon, since he seemed to like the salted, dried meat. He forced himself to eat slowly, though all he wanted to do was shovel the food into his mouth. He hoped that Ket was not going to sit on the rocks all day and wait for him. As much as he didn't want Ket alone in the open water, he also didn't want the mer to not take care of himself while he waited for him to return. But if this Baron Forthwell was not going to the mainland today, Eron guessed he might be able to stay on the island at least until tomorrow without having to worry about making excuses.

He had just finished the last bite on his plate when Maeve returned, sweeping into the dim kitchen like a ray of sunshine. "Tub's filling. Nelson is smaller than you, so I pulled out a few of Marcus's things instead. They might be a little big, but we'll make them look decent for your meeting with the baron."

"I'm going to meet the baron?" Eron asked in surprise.

"I'm sure he will want to speak with you," Maeve said, waving her hand. "You would be a guest in his house, after all, and if he owns your whalling vessel, he might have some questions about the shipwreck. Did you get enough to eat, dear?"

"Yes, thank you," Eron replied, pressing his palms together in a grateful gesture. "I really appreciate it."

"No trouble, no trouble," Maeve said airily. "Come with me, we'll get you into the bath."

The bathtub was not any bigger than his own at his home, but it still felt absolutely amazing, and Eron scrubbed at his skin with the ivory soap until he was pink all over. After he got out and dried off, he did a quick shave and brushed his teeth, which he had missed more than he realized, and then he slipped into the simple clothes Maeve had left out for him. He felt better with clean garments and more civilized with a waistcoat over his shirtsleeves. There was a jacket for him to put over it that was definitely too big, but Eron was not about to complain. Clean, dry, and dressed, he headed back into the kitchen where Maeve waited with her own cup of tea.

"Oh, aren't you just a handsome thing," she cooed when he entered, and Eron blushed a bit. "No funny business, of course, I love my Marcus, but you do clean up nice." Maeve held out his boots to him that she had obviously brushed.

"You really didn't have to do that," Eron said as he took them.

Maeve laughed brightly. "Young man, I am much too old for you to be telling me what I can and can't do. Now, get those boots on so we can get up to the big house."

Chapter 7

THE WALK UP TO the baron's manor was not difficult, even carrying his gear, but every step they took made Eron realize how large the house was in comparison to the modest dwellings of the servants. He was not surprised that it needed a small town to maintain its grand exterior and lush lawn, things he was not used to seeing in a city like Port Ceyran. There was an airship on a landing pad nearby. Whereas the airships Eron was used to for whalling and other air travel were simple neutral-colored balloons, this one had a wine-colored balloon with many brass embellishments and a large crest on the side of some kind of hawk in mid-swoop, talons outstretched to catch prey, entwined with a large 'F.' He was pretty sure he had seen that airship before, coming to or from Port Ceyran, or landed at one of the many docks on both sea and land. He couldn't imagine that the baron would want to stay in a dirty, crowded city when he had such a luxurious home to return to.

Maeve chattered at his side, pointing out various features of the house that he only half-paid attention to. His mind kept drifting back to Ket and hoping the little mer was doing all right. Maeve led him around the side of the house to what he assumed was a servants' entrance, where they entered into the largest kitchen he had ever seen. There were at least ten people running around making various meal preparations, and he realized it would not be unlike the crew of a whalling ship in that aspect.

Maeve steered him to a table off to the side and sat him down there before she went to talk to a few of the other servants who were all dressed in the same striped-pattern overcoats that she and Marcus wore. A few of the servants gave him curious glances, and he gave them what he hoped was a friendly smile in return. "Willem is going to let the baron know you are here, and we'll see when he wants to meet with you," Maeve said when she reappeared at his side. "Until then, you can just stay here."

"Can I help?" Eron offered, glancing around at the bustling kitchen.

"You are a guest," Maeve scolded. "You sit. I'll get you a snack." And she was gone again before Eron could protest that she had just fed him breakfast. He glanced around the busy kitchen at the various instruments. He had a basic kitchen in his own apartment, but the fixtures were older and run down, and he rarely used them anyway. Everything in this kitchen gleamed, as if it was shined every day. It was warm, but not overly so; it seemed that the steam power and other heat was piped out of the kitchen pretty efficiently. The advantages of the rich, he thought to himself.

Maeve returned with a glass of milk and a slice of what looked like strawberry bread before telling him to come find her if he needed anything, and then she went about her duties with practiced efficiency. Eron nibbled at the food, which was absolutely delicious, wrapping the last bite in a napkin and putting it in his coat pocket to give to Ket later.

It was nearly noon before a young man, probably in his early 20's, approached him. "Mr. Marcel?"

"Yes," Eron said, straightening up.

"I'm Willem. The baron is ready to see you now," the young man said. "Please follow me. You can leave your things here."

Eron got to his feet, nervously smoothing the borrowed clothes and his hair. He followed Willem from the kitchen, up a flight of stairs to what seemed to be a grand dining room, then out into a long hallway. There were so many rooms; it almost looked like the building most residents in Port Ceyran lived in, but he was quite sure that the closed doors of this place did not lead to over-crowded, run down apartments. The walls were decorated with patterned wallpaper that did not appear to be new but was well-maintained. The carpet beneath his feet was plush, and he could smell the faint scent of lavender tea coming from it as they walked. Every few steps, there was a console or a side table with something on it. A vase of fresh flowers. A sculpture made from some sort of marble. An eccentric-looking art piece that he thought might be a fish made from various wires and gears. Paintings hung on the walls: beautifully detailed landscapes, portraits of people he did not know, heavily ornamented airships. They passed through what he assumed was the main entryway, with a grand staircase that swept upward to the second floor, splitting at the top to the left and right. There was a chandelier of surprisingly delicate-looking wrought iron hung overhead, and what had to be hundreds of tiny oil lamps burning on it. Eron felt a pit in his stomach as he realized it would be run on oil made from the fat of the whalls.

Willem led him down another hall, taking a few turns until Eron was quite unsure where he was within the structure, before stopping in front of a grand pair of double doors that were currently closed. He tapped his knuckles lightly on the wood. "Enter," came a deep voice. Willem opened the door and moved aside for Eron.

The room he stepped into looked like it was probably a private office or library, with a grand desk on one side, and shelves of books and papers lining the other walls. The oil lamps burned brightly, and there was a fire burning low in the mantle across the room, since the room seemed to be a pleasant temperature right now.

The man at the desk was large, with broad shoulders and a heavy belly underneath his brocaded waistcoat. He looked to be in his late fifties or early sixties, with bushy black muttonchops on the sides of his face. They connected to dark hair on the sides of his head, but the dome of his head was bald. The buttons on his waistcoat gleamed bright gold in the lamplight, embossed with the same diving bird crest that was on the airship. "You're dismissed," the man said, and Willem bowed his head and quickly left, closing the door behind him.

Eron hesitated, but the man beckoned him forward without looking up. Eron could see he had several large rings on each hand.

He moved over to the desk, and the man motioned to one of the wingback chairs there. "Sit."

Eron sat in the leather chair that was smooth and supple under him. The man folded his hands on the desk, then finally lifted his head to gaze at Eron over them. "Eron Marcel, Sky Diver First-Class, is it?"

"Yes, sir," Eron said, not sure if 'sir' was appropriate for a baron or not, but he hoped it was. The man before him did not seem to be the kind who would take lightly to any sort of disrespect.

The man looked him up and down, and Eron felt like he was a prized animal being judged. He tried very hard not to shift under the intense gaze. "Baron Thaddeus Forthwell. I assume Ms. Wilder-Smith told you as such."

"Yes, sir," Eron said again.

"Your name is on record as being lost in a whalling accident nearly a week ago."

"Yes, sir," Eron said. He wasn't sure if he was expected to elaborate beyond that, so he added, "I nearly drowned, but I was res-" He cut himself off. It would be prudent not to mention the mer to this man yet. "I managed to find a rock outcropping, where I stayed for several days."

The baron looked like he was attempting to look sympathetic, but it was a very weak attempt that did not fool Eron for a moment. "We are glad to see you returned safely," Forthwell said in a tone that sounded like he did not much care either way. "I see you are not married, and your sister is your next of kin. I will have you write out a message, and my manservant, Styles, can send it for you."

"Thank you, sir," Eron said, bowing his head in a grateful nod. "I should probably contact my airship crew as well."

Forthwell waved his hand. "We'll take care of that. After they pick you up, are you prepared to go back to work?"

Eron blinked in surprise at the abrupt question. "Well, sir, I actually wanted to talk to you about th-"

"If you need time off to recover, you will receive half-payment for the time you are gone," Forthwell said, and Eron gritted his teeth.

"I actually wanted to talk to you about the whalls, sir."

"What about them?" the baron said in his dismissive way, as if someone as simple as a sky diver could have anything of interest to say.

Eron swallowed hard, feeling his mouth go dry. "While I was traveling back to safety, I learned that the whalls serve a purpose."

"Of course they do," Forthwell said with a chuckle. "They give us oil, whall bone, and hide."

"No, sir, besides that," Eron said. Forthwell gazed at Eron over his hands. Eron waited for permission to go on, but he did not receive it, so he just pushed forward. "There are creatures in the water that rely on the whalls for protection from predators."

"What kind of creatures?" Forthwell asked, raising one dark brow.

Eron licked his dry lips. "A... type of fish." He mentally apologized to the mer for the reduction to mere fish. "And I found that they are in danger. Without the protection of the whalls, they won't survive."

Forthwell gave a shrug of one meaty shoulder. "Survival of the fittest out there."

"No, sir, you don't understand," Eron said. "These are not just ordinary fish. They are intelligent, and perceptive, and... and sentient."

Forthwell's eyebrow quirked again. "Are you telling me that you spoke with a fish, Mr. Marcel?"

"No, sir, I... I mean... Yes, sir." Eron felt his cheeks burn as he stumbled over himself, not sure how to answer the question without really answering it.

"Well, which is it, boy? Yes or no?"

Eron bristled at being called 'boy.' He was younger than the baron, but he was not a child to be talked down to. "Yes," he finally forced out.

The baron looked surprised for just a moment, but it quickly seemed to fade into amusement. "And what did this fish say to you?" he said, as if Eron were no more than an imaginative child.

Eron gritted his teeth, trying to force himself to remain calm. "Without the protection from the whalls, their species would be wiped out."

Forthwell looked at him over his folded hands for a moment. "What purpose do these... sentient fish serve?"

Eron blinked. "What?"

"What do they do? What makes them worth saving?"

"They're intelligent," Eron said, realizing he was repeating himself but not having a better answer to the question. "They know the seas, and they can communicate with the whalls."

Something sparked in the baron's dark blue eyes, and Eron's stomach clenched. "Do they, now? How can they do that?"

"I... don't know," Eron admitted. "I think it's some sort of shared language. But I can't understand it."

"But you can understand these fish?"

Eron was sure he was sounding more and more mad with every word. A week ago, he wouldn't have believed himself either. "No, sir. Not words, at least. But body language, and the way their ears move."

The baron's dark eyebrow flicked upward for the briefest moment before settling again. "I see," he said. "Can all of these fish communicate with the whalls?"

"I believe so," Eron ventured. "But I've really only seen the one do it for any length of time."

"Mm." The baron seemed to ignore him for a moment, his blue eyes rolling up to look at the office ceiling. Eron could only hear the crackle of the fire and the creak of leather as he shifted uncomfortably in his seat before the baron turned to him again. "Well, you've given me something to think on, Mr. Marcel," he said. "It will be a few days before I return to the mainland, at which time we can return you as well. In the meantime, please enjoy our hospitality here, as my guest."

Eron swallowed hard, feeling like he was a chicken being asked to stay in a fox den, but he nodded slowly. "Thank you, sir, I appreciate that very much."

The baron nodded, then reached over and pushed a button on his desk. Only a moment later, the door opened, and another servant entered with a bow. This man was tall and broad-shouldered like the baron, though with much less stomach. His jaw was very round, and he gazed at Eron with dark eyes that glittered in a way that reminded Eron of a hidden animal waiting to ambush prey. "This is Styles. Please, show Mr. Marcel to a guest room," Forthwell said, running his fingertips down his chin. "He may wish to send a message to his sister. He will return to Port Ceyran on my next trip, the day after tomorrow."

"Yes, your lordship," Styles said, his voice low and gruff. "Come, sir."

Eron stood up, taking a few steps toward the door before thinking better of it, turning, and giving the baron a small bow like Willem had done earlier. "Thank you, your lordship," he said, as formally as he could. The baron waved his hand, already absorbed in something he was reading. Eron headed out of the office without another backward glance.

Styles led him a guest room on the second floor, where his bag had already been emptied, the clothes hung up, and the other items placed neatly on the desk.

"There is paper and ink in the drawer," Styles said, waving one beefy hand. "Write out any messages you wish to send, and I will take care of it when I return."

"Thank you," Eron said, nodding gratefully at the man, who seemed more than a little bored with him. Styles nodded, turned sharply on his heel, and left before Eron could say anything more.

He sat down at the desk and wrote out a note to his sister, Emma, letting her know he was alive and well and apologizing for any distress she might have endured. He promised he would be back on the mainland soon and would come to see her once he returned. He sent all of his love to her, Michael, and his niece, Faith. He would have to make it more of a priority to spend time with her. He supposed a near-death experience would make him appreciate his family even more. Even though he couldn't introduce them, he thought that

Faith would like Ket. Ket seemed the playful sort, and he and Faith would probably have lots of fun exploring different objects.

He wrote out another note to his crew, giving them the brief explanation of his survival that he had given the baron. He wondered if Risse was all right. If his best friend was dead or injured, Eron would blame himself, as he had gotten Risse the whalling job in the first place. He realized he should have asked Baron Forthwell.

When Styles returned a little later, Eron handed him the notes and asked if the man could find out what happened to the rest of the crew of the SERENITY. Styles nodded and left again with barely a word, and Eron was once again on his own for most of the afternoon. He took a long, much-needed nap on the comfortable bed until the evening meal was delivered to his room. He had wondered if the baron would ask him to join him for dinner, but he had not, and Eron was grateful for that. Thaddeus Forthwell was not someone he particularly wanted to be around very much. They lived in two entirely different worlds, despite the whalls that connected them.

Dinner was one of the best meals he had ever eaten, everything richly seasoned and perfectly cooked. Eron was also delighted that there was a bowl with fresh apple slices, adding a few of those to the strawberry bread in his pocket for Ket.

One of the servants came to retrieve his dinner tray and delivered him a short note that simply read, "*William Westley deceased. All other SERENITY crew members alive and accounted for.*" Eron felt his heart surge in his chest. Risse was alive, which was a huge weight off his chest. But William was gone. Fuck, he had known William for years. Eron was not one for crying very often, but he did allow a few tears now to fall in the silence of the room, stuffing the folded paper into the pocket of his borrowed coat.

The sun had just started to descend toward the horizon when he rolled up one of the blankets from the bed and draped it over his shoulder. He had been thinking about Ket all day, wanting to know that the mer was safe, especially so close to the mainland and all of the whalling ships. He slipped out of the guest room and headed silently down the hall. He found a set of stairs and took them down, not sure if it was the same ones he had come up earlier in the day. This house was larger than his whole apartment building.

The manor was not entirely silent as he walked; he could hear people moving around and talking in various rooms, and there was the low, constant thrum of what was probably the desalination machines that produced the steam that would control most of the house's functions and created fresh water. He turned several corners before finding himself in an unfamiliar hallway. He turned around, backtracking his path. He took the other hallway he had bypassed before, looking for anything familiar, and then nearly smacked into someone who was coming around the corner at the same time. "I'm sorry!" he gasped, reaching out his hand to steady the person.

It was a woman. She was not very tall, a few inches shorter than Eron, even in her heeled boots. Her white blouse and leather underbust corset were simple but exquisitely crafted from the finest material he had ever seen, her khaki breeches hugging her legs, with shiny, brown leather boots laced up with buttons to her knee. She had blond hair that was twisted into a simple chignon at the back of her head. She had on bright red lipstick that showed off her prominent lips on her otherwise pale, angular face. Her cold expression only sharpened her features, her dark blue eyes hard. "Who are you?"

Eron quickly pulled his hands back as if the woman had burned him. "I'm sorry," he said again. "I'm a sky diver. I'm staying here until the baron goes to the mainland."

The woman's eyes narrowed just a bit, her lips curving into a small smile that did nothing to improve her harsh appearance. "Ah, yes, I did hear about that." She held out one small, white hand. "Lady Lyla Forthwell."

"Oh! You must be the baron's daughter?" Eron said. She did not look much like her father except for the eyes.

Lyla let out a single derisive snort. "Of course," she said in the same dismissive tone that the baron had used. He quickly took her hand and gave the back a polite kiss, noting that her nails were the same bright red as her lipstick.

"I am pleased to meet you, your ladyship."

Lyla laughed, but it was not a warm sound. "Where are you headed so quickly, Mister...?"

"Marcel," Eron said quickly. "Eron Marcel. I was actually looking for the side entrance where I came in earlier today."

"Ah," Lyla said. She gestured over his shoulder. "Back that way, take the second right. The dining room will be on your left, take the stairs down to the kitchen."

"Thank you, your ladyship," Eron said, giving her a polite bow. Lyla waved her hand in dismissal, and Eron took the opportunity to quickly hurry away. Maeve had mentioned the baron's daughter was 'odd.' He understood the feeling. Something about Lyla unsettled him, though he couldn't put into words what it was.

He passed through the empty dining room, then down the stairs and into the kitchen. There were still a few servants bustling around, cleaning and prepping for the morning, but it was not as busy as when he had arrived. "May I borrow this?" he asked, gesturing to one of the oil lanterns by the door.

An older man who was busily polishing silver waved his tarnished cloth in acknowledgement, which Eron took to mean yes, so he picked up the lantern and lit it, trying hard not to think about the whall oil inside of it. It was not completely dark outside yet as he exited the house onto the path to the town, so he turned the light down low to conserve the fuel. The walk to the houses was relatively quick, and a number of people were sitting outside their homes or standing along the streets talking. Eron slowed his pace so he didn't draw too much attention to himself. Several people turned to look at him, and he gave them a nod of his head in return. He had already prepared a story that a few of his personal items had become lost and he was going down to the shore to look for them, in case anyone asked where he was going, but most seemed content to give him a polite smile or wave in return before going back to their conversation. He passed by Maeve and Marcus's house; Marcus was outside with another man, both smoking pipes, and he could see Maeve through the kitchen window talking to another lady who sat at the same table where he had eaten breakfast.

Each step after that took him further down toward the water, the sounds and smells and lights of the town growing fainter with each step. By the time he reached the beach, the sun had vanished over the horizon, and the sky was rapidly turning a dark blue, not unlike Ket's scales. He turned up the lantern light and held it so he could carefully pick his way along the sand and loose brush until he was at the mouth of the cavern he had emerged from earlier that morning. It felt like so long ago. He had to force himself not to run so he didn't slip on the rocks as he made his way inside, his heartbeat picking up in his ribs. What if Ket wasn't there? What if the mer had decided to take his leave now that Eron was safely amongst humans again? What if he had been hurt or killed as he waited off the island for nightfall, perhaps by a shark or other opportunistic hunter looking for prey?

He lifted his lantern as high as he could to throw the light in the dark cave, the sound of the water lapping at the rocky edge becoming louder and louder, but he could not see anything that looked like a mer in the murky glow. A few more steps, and he could see the edge of the water where Ket had been sitting earlier that morning when he left him. There was nothing there now. His heart pounded harder, and he sucked in a sharp breath. He swung the lantern around to look but saw nothing along the whole ledge. His heart gave a sorrowful flutter in his chest. "Ket?" he called, his voice almost overpowered by the lap of the waves near his feet.

There was silence except for the water. Eron felt heat burn in his eyes, but he pushed it back. Ket was gone. He hadn't waited, he hadn't returned. Or he had been too late, and Ket had grown bored waiting and left him. He sighed, his heart feeling like a ballast in his chest, dragging him down. He turned and started to walk back the way he came before a sudden splash came from behind him, followed by a screech and several familiar-sounding clicks. Eron whirled around to see Ket's head and shoulders poking out of the water, and he gasped in relief. He set down the lantern and blanket and hurried to the edge, the water lapping at the toes of his boots.

He suddenly was tackled by a wriggling mer, along with a splash of water as Ket leaped at him, letting out a delighted-sounding squeal as his arms wrapped around Eron's neck. Eron held him close, now soaking wet but not caring as he buried his face in the juncture of Ket's neck. "Hi," he moaned into Ket's shoulder, and the mer gave a series of excited-sounding clicks, his ear fins brushing lightly against Eron's face as they embraced. Ket smelled of briny salt water and sunshine. He took a few steps back, Ket still in his arms, before sitting on the rocky ground and settling the mer onto his lap. "Was I late?"

Ket shook his head, then opened his webbed hand. Something glittered in his palm. It was a large, round pearl, about the size of a blueberry. Even in the dimness of the lantern, Eron could see the opalescent luster that came off of it. He had hardly ever seen a pearl up close; they were so rare, not something he could have easily afforded for himself. "Wow," he said, and Ket's ear fins flickered in delight. He caught one of Eron's hands in his other one and pressed the pearl into Eron's palm. "For me?" he asked in surprise, and Ket nodded eagerly.

Eron rolled it gently around in his hand, feeling the cool smoothness against his skin. "Thank you," he said. His mind was already dancing with possibilities. But he was getting ahead of himself anyway. "I brought you something too. It's not as nice, but I hope you like it."

Ket blinked curiously up at him. Eron pulled the napkin out, handing Ket the piece of slightly-mashed bread. "This has strawberries in it. I thought you might like strawberries, though these ones are dried."

Ket took the bread, giving it a cautious sniff before looking at Eron. Eron chuckled. "You eat it," he said, pointing to Ket's mouth. "Go ahead."

Ket put the piece of bread into his mouth, looking very confused about what to do with it, rolling it around his tongue until he finally figured out how to awkwardly chew and swallow it. Eron watched him closely. "What do you think?"

Ket wrinkled his nose a little, his tongue snaking between his teeth to try to dislodge some crumbs. Eron chuckled. "Okay, no bread. How about this?" He held up an apple slice for Ket. The mer took it, giving it another curious sniff. Eron pulled out a second slice for himself and held it up for Ket to see before biting into it and chewing very deliberately and with his mouth open, which felt extremely uncouth, but he supposed a mer who ripped apart whole fish wouldn't be too concerned with his table manners. Ket imitated him, biting the apple in half before chewing carefully and swallowing. He blinked, and his ear fins gave a flick of delight as he eagerly stuffed the second half in his mouth. Eron laughed and handed him the other half of his own slice, which Ket eagerly devoured, and then Ket was pawing at his jacket where a third slice still lay. "Hey!" Eron protested as Ket's hand dove into the pocket and pulled out the apple piece. It was gone down Ket's throat before he could even think to say anything more, and then Ket was nosing around his coat, searching for more. Eron couldn't stop a snort of laughter. "Well, I guess you like apples. I will bring you more." At least apples were easier to come by and were amongst the cheaper fresh produce he could easily get in Port Ceyran. If he was going to still see Ket once he was back on the mainland, of course.

Ket nosed around his pockets again before drifting lower, and Eron jumped as Ket's face brushed over his crotch. His cock gave a twitch at that, and he flushed, shifting Ket a little in his lap so the mer would not feel his arousal growing. "I don't have anymore, but I'll bring you more tomorrow."

Ket let out a huff and crossed his arms over his chest. Eron leaned in to press his nose to Ket's. "Silly fish," he teased. Ket pressed his nose firmer against Eron's, and then Ket had shifted so that the end of his tail was more between Eron's legs, giving a light rub against his pants. Eron inhaled, fighting back a moan. "Don't do that."

Ket's little smile turned positively wicked, and his tail only rubbed harder against him. Eron groaned. "Ket..."

Ket clicked at him. Eron jumped as his moan of pleasure echoed off the stone walls. He squirmed a little and lifted Ket off of his lap. His pants were damp where the mer had been resting, and he smirked at the blond. "My clothes are all wet now. I guess I'll just have to take them off."

Obviously that was what Ket had been planning, because he clicked eagerly, pawing at Eron's pants in an attempt to help, but he was not very good at it, and Eron was more than a little concerned the borrowed trousers would end up in shreds. He pushed the mer's hands lightly away. "I got it, horny fish, hold your horses."

Ket blinked, and his look was so innocently confused that it sent Eron into a paroxysm of laughter. "Sorry, human expression. It means, slow down, we'll get there."

Ket rolled his eyes and let out a click of annoyance. Eron raised a brow. "What was that?"

Ket did it again. Eron smirked. "You don't want to take it slow?"

Ket let out another huff. The slit in his fin was visible now, the soft, pink innards shining just a bit in the lantern light. Eron leaned over and tipped Ket's chin up with one finger. "Is that so?"

Ket suddenly leaned his head down and nipped at Eron's fingertip playfully. "Ouch!" Eron said, though the response was more automatic than because of actual pain. Before he could think about it, his hand moved, his palm connecting with the slick scales of Ket's tail at the curve of one hip. Ket had looked worried at his exclamation, but as Eron's hand landed on him, he jumped, eyes wide.

Eron flinched, quickly pulling his hand back, guilt washing over him like a tidal wave. "Oh my god, I'm so sorry, Ket!" he gasped. "Are you all right? I didn't mean to do that. Did I hurt you?"

Ket stared at him for a long moment, his golden eyes unreadable, and Eron wondered if he had frightened the mer with his instinctive reaction. But then Ket slowly reached down, picking up Eron's hand in his own and lifting it back to his mouth. His eyes did not break contact from Eron's as he slid one of Eron's fingers past his lips and gave it a surprisingly gentle but very deliberate nip. It hurt just a bit, but the mer's conical teeth didn't break his skin. Eron stared back at him. When he didn't move, Ket gave the finger another soft bite, then shifted a little on his lap to expose more of the length of his tail to Eron.

It took him a few more seconds, but then the air left Eron's lungs in a *whoosh* of disbelief. "You... you want me to spank you?"

Ket's ear fins flicked eagerly. Eron forced himself not to laugh, instead swallowing hard as heat went straight to his dick. "Um... I can do that. I won't hurt you?"

Ket's ear fins gave a flick that he recognized as 'no.' Eron gazed down at the fish tail in his lap. "How do we do that?"

Ket shifted to stretch out, the bend of his waist curled over one of Eron's legs so his tail lay across Eron's lap, the end of it flicking idly. Eron could feel the muscle beneath the scales. Ket was lithe and supple, but as pretty as the tail looked, it was not fragile. He supposed it couldn't be, as the mer's source of mobility. He probably wouldn't do any real damage to Ket if he did spank him, and it had been Ket's idea. Eron hesitantly ran a hand down the curve of Ket's tail that was the widest part of it. "Here?" he asked, and Ket's ear fins flicked. "Okay, this is officially the weirdest thing I have ever done," he said, and Ket gave him a playful smirk, fluttering the fins at the end of his tail in Eron's face. Eron sputtered and shoved them aside. "Hey, cut that out!"

Ket let out an annoyed, little huff. Eron gave him a very light smack that even he knew the mer barely felt, and Ket looked at him with a frown. "What?" Eron said, and Ket gave a pointed wiggle on his lap that ground the side of his tail against Eron's groin. Eron sucked in a breath, his hips pushing toward the delicious, damp friction before he raised his hand and brought it down with a smack that echoed off the cave walls. His palm stung as it connected with the scales of Ket's tail, and the mer jumped, letting out a silent cry. Eron ran his hand soothingly over the spot. "All right?"

Ket nodded eagerly, his ear and tail fins flicking. Eron raised his hand again, and Ket stared at him expectantly. Eron stared back at him. That was more fun than he had expected it would be, and now he was curious to see what he could do to drive the little mer crazy.

When his hand did not move, Ket let out an irritated click. Eron gazed sternly back at him. "Don't get mouthy with me," he said, putting extra gruffness into his voice. Ket blinked, then giggled at his words, and Eron smacked him again, harder. Ket gasped and jumped, and Eron delivered a second swat to the exact same spot before running his hand over it gently. Ket let out a mewling sound that Eron hadn't heard before, and he grinned. "Yeah?"

Ket wriggled eagerly, and Eron felt warmth against his leg. He glanced down to see that Ket's slit was wide open now, the clear liquid shimmering on the front of his scales. Eron only hesitated for a moment before he shifted the mer in his lap so he could undo his pants to free his straining dick. Ket blinked at him. Eron slid his hand down to cup Ket's chin, putting more force behind the grip than he normally would. "I'm going to fuck you while I spank that gorgeous tail, and I'm not going to stop until you can't remember your own name."

Ket's pupils were blown wide as he sucked in a breath, his ear fins giving the tiniest little 'yes' quiver. "Tap me twice if you want to stop, okay?" Eron said, brushing the pad of his thumb over Ket's lower lip.

Ket let out a snort but nodded. Eron gave the rounded part of his tail another smack, and Ket flailed a little, letting out a silent yowl. Eron took that moment to shift onto his back, adjusting Ket until the mer's wet hole pressed against his straining cock. He shifted his hips and slid deep inside. Ket arched, his eyes rolling back in his head just as Eron gave his tail another echoing spank. Ket screeched soundlessly, his insides contracting around Eron's dick in a way that nearly made him forget how to breathe as he began to piston his hips up and down, moving Ket so the mer was riding atop him. His palm slid down the silky scales again before delivering a lighter slap to them, followed by a harder one. Ket writhed against him, and Eron could feel that warm, clear liquid on the fabric of his pants and his skin. He thrust his hips up again with a soft growl, deep inside Ket, and he felt the mer's cock rub eagerly against his own.

Ket made a mewling noise, jerking against him and then back again, trying to push into Eron's open hand, but Eron held him firmly in place, taking a moment to eagerly thrust his hips up and down inside the mer. Ket's back arched, his tail going a little more rigid as the slender muscle of his cock slid out to rub against Eron's with each movement, and Eron could feel the wetness building inside of Ket's heat. He gave an extra hard thrust up into him, feeling Ket's dick jump as he did, and he gave the tail another smack. Ket screeched silently, writhing against him. One more slap of his palm on scales, and Eron felt the hot gush of liquid over his skin as both Ket's hole and his cock spilled over him, clenching around his throbbing dick so tightly it felt like he might break. As Ket's hole pulsed eagerly, Eron grabbed Ket's hips and thrust wildly up into him, his only care being the need to empty himself inside of the mer. Ket was yowling and screeching and writhing, and Eron loved watching every second of it as his cock overstimulated the mer until he yanked Ket sharply down and spilled himself inside him. The world fell away, the only thing silence and the slippery heat of Ket's body against his as he pumped his hips, coming inside of Ket so hard he almost lost his vision, every muscle and fiber rigid with pleasure.

And then the world slowly came back, the lap of the waves nearby, his own labored breathing, Ket's exhale against his chest. He clutched Ket to him, positive he would not be able to move right now if his life depended on it. He just held the mer, trying to find his breath, jerking as Ket's hole spasmed around his cock, making him let out a cry of sensational pleasure. Other than that, and the rise and fall of his chest, Ket had gone completely still on top of him, his cheek resting against Eron's shirt, his webbed fingers clutched into the fabric beneath him.

He wasn't sure how long they stayed like that, but eventually his softening dick slid free of Ket's body, and the mer's cock retreated into his slit again. "Ket?" he asked. The only response was the thump of Ket's tail fin once against his leg. Eron knew he would be in all kinds of pain if he fell asleep on the rocks like this, but he did not care. This was the only place he wanted to be, with the tiny mer cuddled into his arms in his catatonic post-coital bliss. He felt the tail fin brush lightly against him again as he groped for the nearby blanket, pulling it haphazardly over them both before he fell asleep, lulled by the lap of the water and the warm mer snuggled against his chest.

Chapter 8

He was correct that he was going to hurt from sleeping on the rocks. Eron groaned and shifted, blinking hazy eyes to see pink sky shining in at the two entrances of the cave. He had woken up spooned around Ket, who was curled with his back to Eron's chest, snoozing peacefully. Eron sighed silently. He didn't want to leave him, and it sounded like the baron was not planning to go to the mainland today, so hopefully he could take some time to come up with an idea on how to stay with Ket. There had to be a way. Ket could be on land, but it wasn't like Eron could just keep him in his bathtub in his apartment forever. Could Ket even survive in fresh water instead of salt? There was so much he didn't know about the mer. But he wasn't even sure Ket would agree to such an arrangement. And, of course, there was the whole problem of people not knowing the mer existed.

Ket stirred a little, and Eron ran a hand through the mer's hair. Ket settled back into sleep, and Eron leaned down to kiss his shoulder. Ket's ear fin fluttered a bit against his cheek, making him smile. He would love to feel that soft brush every morning. He didn't want to get up, but he was becoming very aware of a rock jutting into his ribs and the coldness seeping into his body. He sat up, stretching every which way until he did not feel like he had just fallen out of an airship. Tonight when he came back, he was bringing a whole goddamn mattress with him if he could. He wondered if Ket would sleep on something soft like a bed. The mer had always slept on the rocks when he'd seen him sleep, and he couldn't imagine there were a lot of comfy napping spots under the water.

Ket yawned and stretched, and Eron ran a hand gently over his tail. "Hey. Wake up."

Ket let out an annoyed huff and opened only one eye to look at him. Eron brushed a piece of hair off the mer's forehead. "Come on, lazy fish."

Ket made a hissing sound, rolling over, taking what little blanket Eron had had with him, burying himself underneath it. Eron laughed. "You can keep that for now. But I should get back to the house soon."

Ket sighed and poked his head out from under the blanket, looking sad. Eron leaned down to press their noses together. "I promise I'll be back tonight," he said firmly. "And I'll bring you more apples."

Ket seemed to perk up at that, sitting up a little, the blanket still draped over his head like a hood. Eron smirked. "Thought that might interest you." He pulled Ket onto his lap, the mer's skin and tail warm against his own. "Can we talk for a minute? About us?"

Ket nodded slowly and nestled into his arms, the blanket still wrapped around him. Eron swallowed hard, tucking Ket's head under his chin. "I can't really know exactly what you're thinking, but I don't want to do anything that you don't want, or put you in danger. With your people, or the whalls, or anything." Ket's face fell just a little when Eron mentioned the whalls, and he quickly shook his head. "I promise my whall hunting days are done. I'll give the baron my resignation today." Ket beamed, his lips pressing to Eron's, and Eron held him close for a moment. At least nearly dying on a whall hunt was an easy excuse for him to want to walk away from the profession. "I don't know what needs to happen to keep you and the other mer safe, but I'm willing to do what I can."

Ket's face lit up, and Eron felt his heart warm. "Would you help me with that? And maybe trust me to tell a few people about your existence? Only people I know who might be able to help protect you?"

Ket hesitated for a moment, and Eron stroked his cheek. "We don't have to decide that now. Just think about it." He swallowed hard, suddenly feeling like he had a mouthful of sand. "But I want to know what you want too. With me. With whatever this is between us. When I go back to the mainland tomorrow, I don't know what my life will look like if I'm not a whall hunter anymore. It's a chance for a new start, anywhere I want to go, anything I want to do. And I... I really like you, Ket. A lot. I don't know a lot about you or your kind, but I'd like to learn more. As much as I can, if you'll let me." Ket stared solemnly back at him. "But if you can't be with me, or don't want to, I understand. I'd be sad to see you go, but I want you to be happy and safe. I'm sorry, I'm not explaining myself well." He could hear himself stumbling, and he flushed, lowering his eyes to the ground beneath him.

Ket's lips pressed gently to his, the mer's hands cupping his cheeks. Eron held him close, so close he could feel the thrum of Ket's heart against him. After a moment, Ket pulled back and glanced behind them at the lapping waves, then back to Eron. His large, amber-gold eyes looked slightly sad, and Eron inhaled. Ket motioned to his temple, then made a lowering motion with his hand. "You'll decide by tonight?" Eron guessed, and Ket's ear fins flicked in assent.

"That's fair," Eron said, stroking his hair. " And, no matter what you decide, I will always be grateful for you saving me."

Ket rubbed his head under Eron's chin, holding tightly to him. Eron sat like that for a long time until the sunlight filled the cave with warmth. "I have to go," he said finally. "I don't want anyone to look for me and find you."

Ket nodded and reluctantly slid off him and into the water that lapped at the shore. Eron folded up the blanket and set it behind one of the nearby rocks so it wouldn't be easily seen if someone did come into the cave. "I'll be back tonight, I promise." Ket waved his tail fin at him, resting his chin on his arms as he watched Eron turn and walk away.

Eron's heart was heavy as he trudged up the path to the baron's estate. The thought of losing Ket was an ache in his heart that he had not felt before. He had so rarely been attached to anyone, with the uncertain nature of his job, but now the thought of not having that tether to Ket felt wrong.

He ran his fingers over the pearl in his pocket. With something as valuable as that, he could make a life for himself and Ket, somewhere away from here, away from the whalling ships and the monsters of the deep. But he did not want to ask Ket for more pearls; the last thing he wanted was the mer to think he was taking advantage of him, using him to find valuable things. But with his savings and selling the pearl, he might be able to afford a small houseship, just for the two of them.

He pushed open the door of the kitchen, walking inside the humid room that smelled of sugar and some sort of vegetable. "Eron!" came a call as he headed for the stairs, and he turned to see Maeve at a counter, rolling out some sort of pastries. He moved over to her.

"Good morning."

"Good morning," Maeve said, giving him a bright smile. "Where did you disappear off to last night?"

Eron shrugged. "Just went for a walk down by the water."

Maeve wrinkled her nose slightly. "You do smell a little fishy."

Eron flushed, glancing down at the borrowed clothing, which had some sand stains now, as well as salt marks from the sea water, and he realized now that he did indeed smell like he had slept down by the water's edge all night. "Shit, I'm sorry, Maeve," he said.

Maeve laughed and shook her head, a few strands of hair flying free from her bun. "No trouble, it will clean up just fine. Go take a bath, and I'll talk to Lettie about finding some different clothes for you."

"You're too good to me," Eron replied with a grin.

Maeve rolled her eyes before she clapped her floury hands together. "What are you up to today?"

"I was going to talk to the baron," Eron said slowly. "I have decided to resign from whall hunting."

Maeve nodded knowingly. "It's a dangerous job. And I suppose you had quite the scare."

"Yes," Eron agreed. "I am ready for something new."

Maeve began to fold the pastry into a series of small dumplings. "Well, I won't keep you. But leave those clothes in your room, and I'll grab them to wash before I head home this evening."

"I can do it," Eron offered, but Maeve waved her hand, a tiny blizzard of flour landing on Eron's shoulder.

"Absolutely not!" Maeve replied sternly. "I'll go talk to Lettie now. Go take a bath before you make my apple dumplings taste like fish."

"Yes, your ladyship. Oh, could I buy a few apples from you?" Eron asked, remembering his promise to Ket. "I really like them. I'll put some Struck in the coat pocket?"

Maeve nodded. "Two Struck, and I'll put four apples on the desk when I pick up the clothes."

"Thank you, Maeve," Eron said, giving her a grateful smile before he turned and headed out toward the main staircase to try to find his way to his room. It took him several minutes of searching and backtracking, but eventually Eron found his guest room and let himself in with a sigh. He grabbed two Struck coins from the pouch that had been with the emergency pack and dropped them into the pocket of his borrowed jacket before sliding it off and hanging it on the wall hook. He pulled off the rest of the clothes and folded them neatly, making sure he removed the pearl from the waistcoat. Finding a robe in the bathroom to wear, he took a long, leisurely bath, letting the heat soothe his sore body.

After his bath, Eron returned to the bedroom to find the borrowed clothing gone, another set in its place, and a tray of food and a plate with four apples waiting for him. He slid on the simple shirt, pants, and waistcoat, guessing they were pieces from another servant's wardrobe, but they were comfortable and fit decently well. He ate the food left for him and packed the apples into a blanket to bring with him that night when he returned to Ket.

Once he was presentable, he rang the bell, and Willem appeared shortly. Eron told him he wished to speak with the baron, and Willem nervously left to deliver the message. He was back a short while later, saying that the baron would meet Eron in the drawing room for afternoon tea, and he would be back to escort him then.

Eron retrieved the pearl and slid it into his waistcoat pocket, his fingers tracing over it lovingly as he sat down to think. Would Ket want to stay with him? It would be a strange life, he was sure of that. Ket had presumably lived his entire life, however long or short it had been, in the sea. Even if Eron found a way for them to live on the water, it would still be an adjustment for both of them. What if Ket didn't want to stay with him? Could they be friends? Eron thought that would hurt, to see Ket once in a while, but not know if he was safe the rest of the time they were apart. He had not seen any of the monstrous creatures when they had traveled from the grotto to the island, but the sea was vast and deep, so much more than the sliver he had seen. And if the whalls continued to be hunted and killed, and the mer scattered, he could never truly know where Ket was or if he was alive.

Later that afternoon, Willem returned to escort him to the drawing room, which had cozy armchairs with a low, round table between them where an elaborate tea setting had been laid. Eron smiled to himself upon seeing the bright copper tea kettle. That was one thing he would want to get for Ket if the mer stayed. Ket had gotten him so many things, Eron was feeling the need to give him shiny gifts in return.

Baron Forthwell entered in a bluster of black and red brocade, and Eron rose to his feet, bowing politely to the man. "Good afternoon, your lordship."

"Good afternoon," the baron said, sitting down in another armchair and pulling out a pipe that he lit while Willem poured tea for them both. Eron took the proffered cup, and he and the baron were silent until Willem had gone, leaving only the two of them in the room.

Forthwell puffed his pipe, and a waft of vanilla and tobacco filled the area. "Now, Mr. Marcel, I'm assuming you had some business to discuss, as this does not seem like a social occasion."

"Yes, your lordship," Eron said, taking another swallow of tea before setting the cup down. He lifted his eyes to meet Forthwell's own, though he could barely see them through the violet lenses the baron was wearing over his eyes today. "I wish to tender my resignation as a sky diver."

"Really now?" the baron said, giving another fragrant puff to his pipe. "After seven years and earning your First-Class rating?"

"Yes, sir," Eron said. "The whall attack made me realize that this is no longer the profession for me."

The baron let out a grunt. "I am sorry to hear that. Could I persuade you to change your mind?"

"I'm afraid not, sir."

The baron puffed at his pipe another moment. "You do not wish to move up to be an airship captain?"

The thought had occurred to him many times, but Eron had known even before now that he did not want that sort of responsibility over so many lives. "Thank you, sir, but no."

"Shame," the baron mused. "Well, your talents shall be missed. I will be headed to the mainland tomorrow, so you are welcome to come along, and I will deliver you to Port Ceyran."

"Thank you." Eron swallowed hard. "Your lordship, when I spoke to you yesterday, I mentioned that the whalls are protecting other creatures in the sea."

"Ah, yes, your... talking fish," the baron said with an amused chuckle.

Eron flushed. "Yes, sir," he said slowly.

"What is your point, Mr. Marcel?" the baron asked, giving him a hard stare through his purple lenses.

"My point is, can't everything that we currently run with oil be run with steam or gas?" Eron asked.

Baron Forthwell gave a hearty laugh at that, as if Eron had just told a marvelous joke. "Of course, it could. But whall oil is worth so much more."

"You're having the sky divers kill whalls for oil even though you have other options?" Eron said, narrowing his eyes. "Do you not realize that the whalls are the only thing protecting the mer?"

"So what if they are?"

"You're killing them both!" Eron protested. "Without the whalls, the mer will die."

Forthwell shrugged his large shoulders. "Everything dies at some point."

"Eventually there wouldn't be any more whalls or mer," Eron protested. "You'd hunt them both to extinction."

The baron let out another booming laugh that made Eron flinch. "And?" he said. "The fewer whalls there are, the more expensive their products become. And it's not as if we will not use alternatives when there are no more."

"Use them now!" Eron protested. "Use steam power! You don't have to kill the whalls!"

"I will remind you, Mr. Marcel, that you are in my house, eating my food, that I pay for with the Struck that comes from whall hunting," the baron said, his voice suddenly growing lower and darker. "A profession that has been quite lucrative for you, I might add. I am certain that your near-death experience has caused you some trauma, but that is hardly a reason to change our entire economy."

"The mer are intelligent!" Eron said, hearing the desperation rising in his own voice. "But they have limited defenses without the whalls to protect them. We know next to nothing about them. Most people don't even know they exist. *I* didn't know they existed until a few days ago. This is an opportunity for us to learn more about them."

The baron stroked his dark muttonchops for a moment. "I see no point behind it, unless these... mer, did you call them, provide some sort of profit."

Eron's mouth dropped. "Not everything has to be about profit."

Forthwell snorted and tapped his pipe against his lips. "You are not a businessman, Mr. Marcel. You are a sky diver. A foolish one, at that. You would throw away your own self-interest over these fish creatures you know nothing about? You would put your colleagues out of a job? Risk your way of life? For what?"

"Because it's the right thing to do," Eron replied through gritted teeth.

The baron raised a dark brow. "According to you. We haven't even seen these creatures. For all I know, you hit your head when you had your accident, and you have been hallucinating sentient fish since then."

For the briefest moment, Eron wondered if that could be true, but he pushed it back. He was alive, and he knew Ket was real and cared about him. He knew it with every fiber of his being. He opened his mouth to protest, but the baron held up his hand for silence.

"But let's say I believe you, Mr. Marcel. You were a sky diver for many years, and I can respect that. You mentioned these creatures communicate with the whalls," Forthwell said, exhaling another puff from his pipe. "If that is the case, imagine how much easier hunting could become. And much more profitable. You don't have to lose out. I see an opportunity of a lifetime before you now. If what you say is true, and you can communicate with these creatures, who in turn can communicate with the whalls, I would have a business proposal for you. You could be a rich man. No more scrounging or risking your life. A high position in my company, stocks, a private place to live, away from the stink of the city."

The words hit Eron like a punch to the gut. Not because they didn't appeal, but because they did. It was what he wanted. A private life, with Ket, away from danger, away from the world, where they could be together, with no one to bother them or hurt them. He couldn't deny the offer was tempting. But, he realized, Ket would never forgive him, and he would not be able to forgive himself. Ket had trusted him with his existence, had trusted him to meet the whalls, to meet other mer. Betraying that trust now would destroy everything that Ket believed about him, and Eron would not have that blood on his hands. Even if Ket decided to stay with his family in the sea and never see Eron again, he could not bring himself to do that to him. "Thank you for the offer, your lordship. But I must decline," he said, getting to his feet and giving the man a small, polite bow.

"Shame," the baron said. "Let me know if you change your mind. Good afternoon, Mr. Marcel."

"Good afternoon," Eron said, giving the man another nod before turning and strolling from the room with as much dignity as he could muster.

Chapter 9

KET WAS WAITING IN the water nearby when Eron arrived at the cave that evening. He tried not to run when he saw Ket peering out of the water just beyond the shore's edge, but he smiled and picked up his steps, and Ket slid onto the rocks and waved his tail eagerly. His heart tap danced in his chest, wondering if Ket had made a decision, but he was not about to push the mer.

"I brought you apples," he said instead, arranging the blankets into a cushion to sit on before unwrapping the fruit and setting it down between them. Ket devoured three of them, begrudgingly letting Eron have one for himself, though Eron gave him the core when he was done, and Ket gratefully wolfed that down too.

"The baron is planning to go back to the mainland tomorrow morning," Eron said as Ket finished the last of the apples. "I'm going on the airship with him to return home."

Ket gazed at him for a moment, then dropped his eyes to the rocks, running his fingers over a few of them. Eron hesitated, then said, "I had an idea. Of how we could stay together." Ket stared at him with wide eyes before his ear fins gave the smallest shiver of anticipation. Eron swallowed hard. "But I need to know what you want first. Because if you don't, I don't want to make y-" He was cut off as Ket suddenly placed a hand over his mouth to stop him talking, and he went silent, staring at Ket in surprise.

Ket reached down to pick up something on the rocks Eron hadn't noticed. It was a rough shell, some kind of mollusk, he guessed. Ket pried open the shell with ease and held it out to him.

Inside the shining nacre, two pink pearls sat on a bed of soft, still-damp seaweed, identical in size, shape, and color. Eron inhaled sharply. "Ket..."

The mer gazed hopefully back at him, and Eron felt heat behind his eyes. "You're going to make me cry, silly fish."

Ket frowned at that, reaching up to stroke Eron's cheek. Eron turned his head to press a kiss to Ket's damp palm before holding out his hand, and Ket placed the shell lovingly into it. It was rough but warm and slightly heavy, the pearls glinting in their little bed of green. "They're beautiful," he breathed, looking up into Ket's eyes.

Ket hesitantly slid over Eron's lap before reaching up to cup his face. Eron held still, letting Ket control the movement even as his heart fluttered in his chest. Ket gazed solemnly at him before lifting up Eron's hand and meshing their fingers together as best he could with the membranes between his fingers. He then leaned in, and his lips pressed to Eron's in a sweet but firm kiss. Eron's breath caught in his throat, and he held Ket close. "All right," he agreed, stroking a hand over Ket's cheek. "You and me together." Ket beamed at him. Eron hesitated for a moment. "Ket… I love you."

Ket let out a screech and threw his arms around Eron, nearly knocking them both over. Eron caught the wiggly mer and held him close, Ket peppering his face with kisses and nose touches until he finally had to push the mer away so he could take a breath. "Wow. Thank you?" Ket giggled and fluttered his ear fins playfully. Eron gave him another kiss. "How do you say 'I love you' in your language?"

Ket let out a series of clicks that ended with a little chirp. Eron raised a brow. "Um, I'm going to have to work on that one."

Ket beamed and repeated the sounds, leaning in to press his nose firmly to Eron's once more. Eron closed the shell with the two beautiful pearls and tucked it into his waistcoat pocket. Just those two pearls alone would be enough for a small airship if he sold them. But he wouldn't. They were a gift from Ket, a promise, and he would not trade them, not for a fleet of airships or a million Struck.

"I hate even asking this, but can you get more pearls?" Eron said softly.

Ket blinked, then flapped his ear fins 'yes,' cocking his head curiously to the side. Eron smiled. "Pearls are really valuable. I won't ever sell these ones, but if you can get more, I can buy a small airship to live on the water, with you."

Ket's eyes went wide, and he let out a delighted-sounding screech that echoed off the cave walls and made Eron's eardrums throb. "I'm guessing you like that idea."

Ket almost jumped into his arms, and Eron held him close, feeling happiness bloom in his chest. Tomorrow he would go back to the mainland, let Emma know he was safe, and then he would work on creating a new life that would be just him and Ket. He would never have imagined that his first time saying "I love you" in a romantic way would be to a half-fish creature that didn't even speak the same language as he did, but he couldn't imagine saying it to anyone else.

He created a little bed with the blankets he had brought from the house, and they made love on them twice that evening. Afterward, the mer curled up next to him, his scales cool and a little rough against Eron's skin as they both drifted off into contented slumber.

A nearby sound roused Eron from sleep, and he blearily lifted his head, only to suddenly be blinded by the light of a lantern in the darkness. He threw up his hand to shield his eyes, hearing heavy footfalls and the crunch of boots on the rocks. Next to him, Ket stirred, fins twitching as he opened his eyes. Eron tried to see beyond the light, but all he could make out was a hulking mass of shadows that was probably several people approaching. "Who are you?" he demanded.

The shapes did not respond. Eron tried to sit up but suddenly found himself pinned to the ground, and something sharp stabbed into his arm. He let out a cry, thrashing underneath the shadowy forms as heat filled his body. He heard a screech and tried to turn toward Ket, but he suddenly felt a thousand times too heavy. He groaned and groped out, trying to find the mer in the scuffle, but his arm felt like it was not attached to him anymore and did not want to respond. He could hear shouts and splashes and noises, but they all sounded very far away. He rolled a little, trying to push himself up, but everything was going fuzzy. He felt like he might throw up, the world tipping on its axis. The beams of light were moving too fast, and his brain was moving too slow. All he knew was that Ket was in danger. He reached out, feeling his fingers barely skim over one wet fin before the world went black.

Eron thought he might have woken up once, opening blurred eyes to see golden light overhead that made his head throb and pinch like it was in a vise. He could hear a thrumming noise, though he couldn't tell what it was. The world tipped again, and he went spiraling back into darkness.

When he woke up again, the floor was cold beneath him, though the same yellowish lamp light stabbed at him through his heavy eyelids. The world swam, and he curled into a ball, trying to focus on something, anything, besides the humid air and the sickly light. His stomach tilted, and he rolled over just in time to vomit onto the floor, sweat breaking out on his forehead and pouring down his neck and back.

"That will pass soon," came a voice nearby, and Eron dragged his head up to see the light reflecting off of a brocaded, black coat and bare head surrounded by dark hair. That was all he could make out before he doubled over and threw up again, his stomach clenching as he fought between emptying his stomach and making it stop. There was the sound of something metal scraping over tile, and he squinted his eyes open to see a cup of water in front of him. He fumbled for it, spilling some of it over his chest as he took a drink and swished some around his mouth to clear the sour taste of bile there.

Once he had caught his breath and the world felt more stable, Eron looked around, then felt his stomach heave again as he saw bars in front of him. He stood up and nearly cracked his head on the ceiling. He winced, ducking his head and moving cautiously forward. He realized as he stared between the cell bars that it was built under a staircase, which was why the ceiling was so low. He gripped the bars and looked out into the bright light.

Wherever he was, it did not have any windows, so he suspected it might be underground. The room beyond the cell was large, so large he thought it might be part of the cellar of the baron's manor; he could barely see the far wall. And what he could see of it was obscured by a variety of shelves, tables, and brass and copper pipes that snaked upward and along the room's ceiling like creeping vines. It almost looked like a factory, or like Risse's factory workshop. There were tools, books and papers with diagrams that he could not make out, and still more things he couldn't even begin to guess what they were.

He saw movement out of the corner of his eye and turned to see Thaddeus Forthwell standing nearby. Next to him, silent and brooding as ever, was Styles, holding a copper pail in his hand.

"How are you feeling, Mr. Marcel?"

Eron ignored the question. "Where am I?"

Forthwell waved a hand around. "My daughter's laboratory. It's quite an honor. Not just anyone gets to see it."

Eron wanted to say something sarcastic, but his brain felt like it was still trying to catch up with him, and he bent over to dry heave again. Once his stomach had decided it was done with that, he started to feel a little better, and he straightened up, grasping the bars in front of him with both hands. "Where is Ket?"

"Where is what?" the baron asked, tipping his head slightly.

"Ket. The mer that was with me," Eron replied, narrowing his eyes. "What the hell have you done with him?"

A sudden splash of stale, lukewarm water hit him full in the face. Eron sputtered as the water sluiced off of him and over the mess on the floor, washing down a small drain at the back of the cell wall. He shoved his dark hair out of his eyes, glowering at Styles, who stood holding the now-empty pail, entirely uncaring. The baron held out a coarse towel through the bars. "Now then. Dry yourself off, Mr. Marcel, and we'll have a talk."

Eron took the towel, giving a few cursory swipes to his face and hair and over his chest and legs before tossing it aside and turning to glare at the baron and his henchman.

"I want to see him," Eron replied, grabbing onto the bars of the cell again.

"You do not give the orders here, boy," Baron Forthwell said sternly.

"Is he alive?"

"For now," the man said, waving his hand dismissively. "Lady Forthwell did have to incapacitate him to examine him, of course."

Eron felt his blood run cold. "What do you mean? Where is he?" Images of Ket flayed open on a table assaulted his mind, and he fought back another mouthful of bile. "What did you do to him?"

The baron ignored his questions. "Now, we have much to discuss."

"How do I know he's alive?" Eron demanded.

The baron chuckled. "I suppose you will just have to trust me."

"Because you are obviously so trustworthy," Eron spat out.

Forthwell stroked his fingers over one of his bushy muttonchops. "You are learning quickly. I suppose I should have expected as much from a sky diver who has lasted seven years. You are quite the example of tenacity, Mr. Marcel."

Eron wasn't sure what he was supposed to say to that, so he went with the first thing that came to his mind. "Go fuck yourself."

Styles suddenly stepped forward and slammed his arm against the bars of the cell, catching Eron's fingers, and Eron let out a yelp, yanking his hands back and curling them protectively to his chest.

Baron Forthwell chuckled mirthlessly. "I don't think you understand the situation here, boy. I own the whalling fleet." His dark blue eyes narrowed in a lascivious grin. "Which means I own the crew to go along with it. And that includes you. Ergo, you will do as you are told."

"Like hell I will!" Eron snapped, suddenly feeling like he had been plunged back into the cold depths of the sea. "I quit the fleet earlier today. You don't own me."

The baron threw back his head and laughed loudly. "Really now? Shall we examine that statement? You are on my private property.

You served on an airship crew that I own, under my employ. And no one knows you are alive, so no one will know to look for you." The baron's smile grew a bit wider. "It sounds like I actually *do* own you."

"But my sister, and my crew. You said you'd contact them."

"Oh yes, I will at some point," the baron said, taking his violet glasses off of his nose and pulling a handkerchief from his pocket to clean them carelessly. "When I feel it is prudent. Whether it is to report you alive or dead is entirely yet to be determined."

Eron felt his blood turn to ice in his veins. "What is it that you want?" he said, hearing the hoarseness in his voice, his fingers still throbbing from where Styles had slammed them.

"I'm glad you are seeing sense," Forthwell said. "Now then. You say that these... creatures can summon the whalls. How do they do that?"

Eron swallowed hard. "I... I don't know," he said. "I didn't see him do it."

"Then how did you find the whall?"

"He led me to it," Eron ventured.

"How did it find it?"

"I don't know."

"How do they find these?" the baron asked, suddenly reaching into his jacket pocket and pulling out the three pearls Ket had given him.

Eron let out a snarl. "Give those back!" He lunged an arm through the bars, trying to snatch them, but the baron was a few steps outside of his reach; Styles stepped forward, grabbing Eron's arm and shoving him sharply backward. Eron stumbled, grabbing for the bars as he flailed but missed them, landing hard on his back, the breath knocked from his lungs.

"I asked, how do they find these?" the baron asked.

Eron rolled onto his side and coughed. "I don't... know..." he managed to wheeze out.

"There seems to be a lot you don't know, Mr. Marcel," the baron said, his voice dropping dangerously.

"Because I don't!" Eron protested.

"And yet you were willing to stick your dick in it," the baron chuckled, rolling the pearls around on his palm. "Do I not pay you enough to find a brothel whore to satisfy your wantonness, or are you just into animals?"

Eron felt his face grow hot, and he scrambled to his feet, barely missing knocking his head on the low ceiling again. "How dare you!"

Both Styles and the baron laughed at that, and Eron felt his skin prickle with angry heat.

"Well, we shall come back to that later," Forthwell said, waving his hand and pocketing the pearls once more. "Why don't you tell me what you do know about these creatures?"

"I'm not telling you shit," Eron snarled.

"You seem to like pain, Mr. Marcel," the baron said with a cold smile. "Just for yourself? Or do you like when it's inflicted on others?"

Eron's heart hammered at that, wondering whom else the baron might hurt to get answers out of him. "Where is Ket?" he demanded again. "I'm not telling you anything until I can see for myself that he is alive and safe."

The baron considered this for a moment, then gave Eron a not-at-all-friendly smile. "Very well, I am a businessman, after all. You see your fish, you will answer my questions, and then we'll discuss what will happen from there." Eron frowned, not sure what that meant, but he was not about to protest further if the baron was agreeing to let him see Ket.

"If he is safe and unharmed, I will."

"Then turn around and put your hands through one of the bars, please," Forthwell said, his tone suddenly much more pleasant.

Eron blinked, but he did as he was told, turning his back to the bars and sliding his hands in between them. He heard someone step up behind him, guessing it was Styles, and something buckled around his wrists, locking them together. His hands flexed, and he realized it was a pair of leather handcuffs with a few links of chain between them, though not enough for him to be able to strangle anyone if he could get his hands around to the front. Then the door of the cell was unlocked, and Eron turned around as Styles grabbed his arm and hauled him out roughly.

"You may be foolish, but I don't think you are stupid, Mr. Marcel," said Forthwell calmly. "No funny business unless you want to end up in a world of pain."

"Yes, your lordship," Eron gritted out.

The baron nodded to Styles, who hauled Eron along as they crossed the room. They passed several tables filled with sharp instruments and bottles full of things he didn't know but decided he did not care to find out. Shelves were full of strange devices, books lay open on surfaces next to piles of notes and journals. Gears, screws, and wires were strewn about, and Eron could see tiny models of things he recognized, including an airship balloon and a desalination tank.

They turned a corner, and Eron stopped so suddenly that Styles nearly knocked him over. Lyla was standing next to a long, wooden surgeon's table. She wore a white lab coat over her outfit, as well as what looked like a leather apron and matching leather gloves. Her back was to him, but when she moved aside, his heart skipped a beat in his chest. Ket was lying on the table, a leather strap buckled over his chest, pinning his arms to his sides, and another was strapped over part of his tail to keep it still. His eyes were open only halfway, and his pupils were so constricted, Eron could barely see them amidst the gold, unsure if Ket could even see anything at all. "Ket!" he gasped, trying to dash over to the table, but Styles grabbed him by his bound wrists and yanked him back, wrenching his shoulders painfully.

"It seems they have two sets of lungs," Lyla commented, though it seemed directed at no one in particular. "Ones for oxygen above the water, and ones that filter oxygen below. Fascinating." Lyla glanced up at him, lifting up the magnifying goggles she had been wearing to rest them on top of her blond hair. Her red lips quirked up into a smile that reminded him of a snake. "Ah, Mr. Marcel, perhaps you can answer a few questions for me."

Eron glowered slightly, until Styles gave him a harsh shake that clacked his teeth together, and he forced out, "Yes, your ladyship?"

"You said it can communicate with the whalls. How does it do that without vocal cords?" Lyla asked.

"How... do you know that?" Eron asked, feeling a little woozy as he scanned over Ket for signs of damage. Other than a few scratches on his arms and tail, there did not appear to be any cuts or dissection marks on him, though several nasty bruises were forming on his throat and his torso.

Lyla rolled her eyes. "I am a scientist, Mr. Marcel. I examine these sorts of things."

Eron gave a small struggle against Styles' grip. "Let me see him," he pleaded. "To make sure he's all right. And then I'll answer your questions, as much as I know."

The baron waved his hand. "Let him see the fish."

Styles let go of Eron's arm so fast, he nearly fell on his face. He stumbled and caught himself against the edge, making the decision to stay on the opposite side of the table as Lyla, with both Styles and her father watching him. "Ket?" he said as he leaned over the restrained mer. "Ket, can you hear me?"

Ket's chest rose and fell steadily, his eyes still half closed. His ear fins gave the smallest of 'yes' flicks, and Eron let out a breath of relief. "What did you do to him?" he demanded, turning to Lyla sharply.

"Just a mild sedative," Lyla replied. "It should wake up shortly. I didn't want to risk too much, since I don't know its anatomy yet."

Eron glowered but turned back to Ket on the table again. "I'm here," he soothed, dropping his voice low. "I'm not going to let them hurt you."

"Now, Mr. Marcel, you have seen your fish and that it is unharmed," Forthwell said, gesturing to a nearby wooden chair. "Please, sit, and let's talk." Eron hesitated, glancing down at Ket again. "Sit, or Styles will make you," the baron replied firmly.

Eron swallowed, then turned and moved to sit in the indicated chair. Styles grabbed his wrists and undid what he assumed was a connecting link, because he found himself locked to the chair by his cuffs. He gave a cursory struggle, but he would not be able to move very fast or very far in a short time. "What does it eat?" the baron asked, raising a brow at him, and Eron blinked at the sudden question.

"What?"

"What does it eat?" Forthwell asked again, pronouncing each word individually like Eron was a child.

"Oh, um..." Eron was about to tell the man that Ket liked fruit and dried meat, but he decided to keep that to himself. "Fish. They catch them and rip them apart with their teeth."

Forthwell nodded to Styles, waving his hand. "I'm sure our guests are hungry. Bring something for Mr. Marcel and his... friend."

Styles grunted in acknowledgement, then turned and walked away. Eron could hear his heavy tread go up the stairs, and he heard what sounded like a door open and shut, and a heavy lock thunking into place. Lyla was writing something in a journal, glancing up at Ket every few moments.

"Why don't you just kill me?" Eron asked after an unbearably long moment of silence.

"I am a scientist, Mr. Marcel," Lyla replied without looking at him, pursing her bright red lips. "I have questions, you have answers. We both want to learn more about these... what are they called... mer?"

"How do you know that?" Eron asked.

Lyla held up something, and Eron's stomach dropped as he recognized the journal with its drawings he had taken from the emergency pack what felt like a lifetime ago. "That's not mine," he ventured. "I found that while I was stranded."

"Ah, I see," Lyla said, setting the journal aside. "Such interesting creatures," she said. "I cannot wait to study them further and find out what makes them tick." She ran one of her leather-gloved hands down Ket's tail.

"Get your hands off of him!" Eron hissed.

Lyla and her father only laughed. "Their anatomy is fascinating. I wonder if they are all the same. I shall have to have a tank built big enough to hold them while I examine them."

"You can't!" Eron protested.

"Can't what?"

"You can't study them in captivity!"

"I am quite certain I can," Lyla said with a cold laugh that set Eron's teeth on edge.

Baron Forthwell shrugged his massive shoulders and let out a chuckle that sounded like a growl. "I suspect they would be easier for the sky divers to catch than the whalls."

"This one may be worth cutting open to find some answers to my questions," Lyla said. "Once I have more live specimens to observe."

Eron heard blood rushing in his ears, and he bared his teeth like a snarling wolf. "I will fucking kill you if you touch him!"

The baron's fist connected with his face, and Eron felt one of his rings slice into his lip, a gush of blood welling inside his mouth and over his chin. "You will watch your language in front of a lady, boy."

Eron wanted so badly to respond, but his mouth and jaw were pounding in pain.

"I will keep this one alive for now," Lyla said, as if her father had not just punched a man bound to a chair a few feet away from her. "I have a feeling it will interact more with your cooperation. And I'd rather have a live specimen than a dead one. But, of course, a dead one can be quite informative as well."

The baron pulled a handkerchief from his pocket and wiped away the drops of Eron's blood from his jewelry. "Now, Mr. Marcel, you have some questions to answer for us."

Eron gave another small struggle, but the cuffs stayed firmly in place, and he was starting to hurt his shoulders. Blood dripped off his chin and onto his shirt. The baron pulled out the pearls from his pocket and examined them again. "How did it find these?"

"I don't know," Eron said hoarsely, forcing himself to speak slowly and clearly through his gritted teeth. "He just brought them to me."

"For what purpose?" Forthwell asked.

"They were a gift," Eron said, hating to admit the words to this man, but at least here he could see Ket and make sure he was not harmed.

"A gift?" the baron asked in amusement. "For what?"

"He collects things," Eron said, deciding he was not about to tell the Forthwells that he and Ket had made a promise to stay together. "He just brings them to me."

"What sorts of things?" Lyla asked without glancing up from where she was making some notes in a journal.

"He found food and fresh water for me when I was stranded," Eron said. "I don't know where, he just came to me with it. He had other things in the cave we were in. It was mostly junk, stuff he probably found in the water."

"Such as?" Lyla prompted.

"Just... stuff," Eron replied. "Bottles. Broken tools. Airship pieces. Things like that."

"Did you ask him to bring you anything specific?" Lyla asked.

"No," Eron replied, remembering that everything Ket had brought to him had been without prompting, even his dive equipment.

Ket's tail suddenly gave a little twitch, and Eron sucked in a breath. "Ket!" he called. The mer's eyes fluttered closed, then open again. Eron yanked at his bonds, but he could not get free of the chair. "Ket, look at me!" he said.

Ket's ear fins turned in the general direction of his voice, seeming uncomprehending of his location. Then his golden eyes, still clouded from the drugs in his system, opened and met Eron's, and he let out a frantic squeak. Eron opened his mouth to tell him to stay still, but the words came too late. Ket wrenched against the leather straps, trying to flail, but Eron could see the leather cutting into the mer's skin. "Ket, stop!" he said. "Stop moving, please! I'm here!"

Ket went limp against the table, chest heaving, his eyes darting frantically around until they seemed to focus on Eron, and he let out a few soft clicks. Eron gave him a weak smile that he was sure looked absolutely horrifying with his bleeding lip. "Hey. Just stay calm, okay? I'm here. I won't let them hurt you."

Ket gave another click, his ear fins flat with fear. "It understands you?" the baron asked.

"Yes," Eron said.

"Does it understand anyone else?"

"I don't know," Eron said begrudgingly.

The baron moved over next to the table and held up one of the pearls in front of Ket's face. "Do you recognize these?" he asked gruffly.

Ket stared at the pearl, then turned his eyes past the man to Eron in the chair. "It's okay," Eron soothed again. "Just answer the question, Ket, please?"

Ket turned amber eyes back up to the baron, his ear fins flicking just a little. "That means yes," Eron said, then gave a yank in his chair as Lyla suddenly grabbed one of Ket's ear fins, swiveling it back and forth. Ket let out a high-pitched screech and snapped his teeth at her, narrowly missing her leather-gloved hand.

The baron's palm landed on the table's surface with a sharp *thwack*, only inches from Ket's face, and the mer froze, eyes wide. Lyla seemed entirely unperturbed by either of them. "If you bite me, I will remove your teeth," she remarked, and Ket let out a soft hiss. Eron had heard Ket's angry hiss before, but this one sounded different. It sounded like fear.

"Leave him alone," he growled, trying to draw the attention back to him.

The baron held up the pearl again. "Could you find more of these?"

Ket looked over at Eron again, who nodded at him. Ket gave his ear fins another 'yes' flick. The baron smiled. "Ah, good. Your other... mer friends, could they find them too?"

Ket gave another 'yes' flick.

Lyla suddenly moved away from the table and over to something tall that was covered with a sheet. She yanked the material off of it to reveal something Eron immediately recognized. It was a desalination tank. The copper and glass tube would be filled with water and then heated, the steam collected for power, the water collected after the salt was separated. Lyla tossed a lever on a nearby panel, and the top of the tube opened. She pressed a button, and a loud rumble sounded before water began to pour into the glass tube from a pipe above it. Sea water, Eron realized as the salty, briny smell hit his nose.

Lyla turned back to the table and adjusted something. The table suddenly rotated until it rested at an angle. Lyla undid the strap holding Ket's tail. Eron expected Ket to thrash, but the mer seemed frozen in fear. Lyla undid the other strap that held Ket's arms and chest. As soon as it was loosened, Ket slid down and hit the tile floor with a thump, skidding a few steps across it on his slick tail. Eron tried to lunge out of the chair, but the leather cuffs held him in place. "Ket!" he cried. Ket turned terrified, amber eyes to him, reaching out a hand in his direction.

Lyla tossed something over him, and Ket screeched. Eron gasped in horror as he realized it was a net. But this net was not rope or other sinew. This net was made of metal, maybe copper or brass wire, woven into a chain link pattern, some of its connection points jutting out in such a way that they hooked into Ket's skin as the mer jerked and struggled. Ket let out a silent scream, clawing and fighting against the net, but his thrashing only tangled it further around himself. "Ket, stop!" he said, trying to be heard over the racket of the rushing water, the metal scraping on the tile, and Ket's powerful tail smacking into the floor. "You're going to hurt yourself!"

Lyla was watching curiously, and Eron saw her lips draw up in a sudden smile. "Ah," she said, making a note of something in her journal. "I see."

"What?" Eron demanded. "Get that thing off of him!"

Ket let out another silent screech before he lay frozen, hopelessly tangled in the wire net. Eron could see several places where blood oozed from scratches and cuts on his skin and tail, the barbed metal digging into him. "I'm here," he tried to soothe the mer, who turned terrified eyes to him from the floor. "Please, just stay still."

Ket did as Eron said, though Eron could see the trembling in his body. He turned to Lyla and the baron again. "Please. Get him out of there, you're hurting him."

Lyla made another note, then turned to her father. "Some of the sounds it makes only carry under water. That's why it was screaming but we couldn't hear it. I suspect that may have some connection to the whalls as well."

Forthwell smiled proudly at Lyla. "If we take this one and put it in the water, perhaps others of its kind will come to try to save it," he said thoughtfully. "We could summon a few of the whalling ships and have divers ready. Then we can catch a whole school of them for you to study, my dear."

Realization dawned on Eron that the net Lyla had tossed over Ket had constricted and wrapped him up so he couldn't move. If the sky divers were able to get nets like those around the mer, they would be helpless. He imagined them all tangled in those sharp barbs, the little baby mer in between their parents, and his stomach dropped like the floor was an airship deck suddenly plummeting beneath him. "Please," he said. "Don't do this." Lyla moved over to study the net. Ket hissed at her as she knelt next to him, another desperate plea of fear. "Please," he begged softly, feeling another gush of warm blood over his chin from his lip. "Get him out of there, I'll do anything."

"This isn't about you, Mr. Marcel," Forthwell replied with a chuckle.

Ket let out a sound that Eron hadn't heard before, a low, keening whine, and it sent pain into the deepest part of him. Ket sounded like a wounded animal caught in a trap. "Perhaps I can figure out how to record their sound for the airships to play back to summon the whalls," Lyla remarked, shifting the barbed net a little with her leather gloves, and Ket let out a pained squeak.

Forthwell grinned. "A fleet of whalls and pearl divers, right on our doorstep," he said.

Eron heard the lab door open and the clunk of footsteps on the stairs. He gave another twist to try to get free of his restraints, but he only succeeded in wrenching his shoulders again. Styles appeared, carrying a tray, which he set on a nearby table.

Lyla smiled at him, leaning over to press a button, and the rush of water into the almost-full tank slowed to a trickle and then stopped. "Ah, Styles, perfect timing. I will pull this net off, and then you can toss the creature in the tank for now."

Styles nodded, and Eron gritted his teeth. Lyla began to unwind the net from Ket with her leather gloves. Ket whined breathily but stayed still. Eron watched as the barbs pulled free from his skin, leaving behind trickles of blood. He wanted to scream and tear Lyla and the baron apart with his bare hands, but he couldn't do anything, trapped in the chair as he was.

Eventually the net came free, and Ket unwound himself from his curled position on the floor, letting out a sound that sounded almost like a sob. Styles reached down and grabbed him by the arm, pulling him across the tiles. Ket screeched, and Eron surged in his chair enough that the feet left the floor. "For fuck's sake, you're hurting him!"

Styles ignored him, pulling Ket up the stairs next to the tank. When he reached the top, he picked him up like the mer was no more than a bag of rice, and unceremoniously dropped him into the tank. Ket fell in with a splash, scrambling to right himself in the water. Lyla pulled the lever, and the large, copper lid of the tube closed and sealed in place.

The tank was so small with the mer in it now. There was no way that Ket would be able to swim around or even really stretch out. Ket slammed his shoulder into the glass of the tube with an audible thump. Eron winced. "Ket, it's okay!" he called. Ket's golden eyes were wide with fear, and his hands slapped at the tank frantically, trying to find a way out. Eron had no idea if Ket could hear him through the glass and sealed lid. The water had already turned a slight pinkish color around Ket from the blood coming off the mer's wounds. That couldn't feel good either, salty sea water in those cuts and punctures.

The baron moved over to the tank, studying Ket for a moment, his hand reaching up to touch the glass, and Ket hissed. Forthwell laughed. "Slippery creatures." He turned to Eron with a cold smile twisting his lips. "I wonder what he sees in you, Mr. Marcel, besides a murderer."

Eron let out a snarl. "I'm not the fucking murderer here. I'd die before I help you kill any more whalls or hurt the mer!"

Both of the Forthwells laughed at this. "You are already dead," the baron said, gazing at Eron over his glasses. "But you know who isn't, yet? Your little fish friend. Let's not forget he is in one of the desalination tanks."

Eron was sure his heart stopped dead in his chest. The desalination tanks were heated to produce steam. The glass and copper structures were built to withstand extreme heat. Unable to escape the tank, Ket would be boiled alive. "Don't!" he said, the word ripping from his throat like a blade through a piece of paper.

Forthwell smiled coldly at him. "You will do what you are told?"

Eron swallowed hard, tasting blood all the way down his throat, and he bowed his head, feeling himself shaking. "Yes," he said softly.

"Didn't quite catch that," Forthwell said, cupping his hand exaggeratedly around his ear.

"Yes," Eron said through gritted teeth.

"Yes, what?" Forthwell asked, like Eron was a misbehaving child.

"Yes, sir," Eron forced out, and Forthwell smirked.

"Ah, there we go. I knew you had some manners somewhere in you."

Eron clenched his lips together to keep from saying something he would regret. Ket's safety was the important thing right now.

"Let us go and arrange for a whalling fleet to arrive here tomorrow morning," the baron said, turning to Lyla. "I'll have the servants gather the nets and prepare them as well." Lyla nodded and removed her gloves and apron, hanging them on a nearby hook.

Eron gritted his teeth, tensing in the chair like he might try to spring out of it, but he knew he was going nowhere. "You can't do this."

"Oh, I assure you, I can," the baron replied. "Styles, feed our guests, and then come assist us."

"Yes, your lordship," Styles said with a bow.

The baron and Lyla headed across the laboratory and up the stairs, vanishing into the house. Eron wanted to scream and thrash and rip the chair he sat on apart, but his rage could not break the metal that locked him in place. Even if he was able to get off the chair, he couldn't do much against Styles or help Ket with his hands locked behind him. They had time, for the little good it would do. He turned to Ket again, who had his hands and nose pressed against the glass, watching him with wide, scared eyes.

Styles picked up one of the platters from the tray, pulling the lid off, and Eron almost instantly was met with the smell of dead fish that had sat in the sun for most of the day. His gorge rose in his throat, and he forced it back down again. He watched as Styles flipped the switch to open the tank lid, then climbed up a short set of stairs. He upended the plate to dump the fish into the water. The dead fish slowly sank vertically down until it hit the bottom and slid to lay flat. Ket wrinkled his nose, giving it a disgusted look. Eron frowned at Styles. "That fish is not fresh."

"Won't get any fresher," Styles grunted as he came back down and closed the tank lid again. He picked up another plate that held a simple dinner roll and a cup of water. He placed it on Eron's lap before turning to walk away.

"Aren't you going to unlock my hands so I can eat?" Eron asked.

"Sounds like *your* problem," Styles said as he tromped off and headed up the stairs again. The door at the top opened and shut, and the heavy lock fell into place.

Eron groaned. He had to be careful not to upset the tray, or he would get nothing. He glanced up at Ket, who was watching him again. "Are you all right?" he asked.

Ket's ear fins flicked just a little. Eron sighed. At least Ket could hear him. "He's right," he pointed out. "That fish is only going to get more disgusting if you leave it."

Ket looked sulky, but he slowly sank down until he was sitting on the bottom of the tank, picking up the fish with two fingers the way someone might pick up a dirty shoe. Eron couldn't blame him; it hadn't smelled good to begin with, and it was probably worse in the confines of the water tank. "I'm so sorry, Ket," he said as the mer gingerly adjusted the fish to take a bite. Ket's eyes met his, and his ear fins flicked. "Did you hear what the baron and his daughter wanted?"

Ket nodded sadly, taking another bite of fish. Eron sighed. "I don't know what to do... I don't want to help them, but I don't want them to hurt you either."

Ket gave him a sorrowful look, toying with one of the fish bones.

"I don't want you to worry about me," Eron said. "If you get the opportunity to get away, you go."

Ket frowned at him, his ear fins wriggling an emphatic 'no.'

"I mean it," Eron said. "If you get in the open ocean, they won't be able to find you. You can tell the other mer and the whalls to hide. Please. I don't want you, or any of them, to die."

Ket glowered and flicked his tail in annoyance. "I'm so sorry," Eron said miserably, heat burning in his face. "I put you in danger. I shouldn't have-"

Ket gave the glass a sharp slap with his palm that made Eron jump. He looked up, and Ket began to click and chirp at him. He had no idea what the words were, but from the look on Ket's face, he suspected the mer was chastising him and telling him not to blame himself. And then he heard a series of clicks and a chirp that he recognized, and he smiled weakly. "I love you too."

Ket beamed at him, then motioned to the tray on Eron's knee before pointing to his own temple and sinking down to sit on the bottom of the tank again. Eron glanced down at the tray on his thighs, trying to figure out the best way to get the food to his mouth without his hands. Damn Styles. He leaned down and lapped at the water in the cup as best he could. He was sure he was going to spill it soon; better to have it be as little as possible wasted. When his tongue couldn't reach the water anymore, he gave up and leaned down to pick up the dinner roll with his teeth. He adjusted it in his mouth, taking a bite and chewing as best he could, nibbling at the roll until it was gone. His stomach still roiled, though he suspected it was the situation, not the drugs in his system anymore. The food and sea water seemed to have cleared Ket's system of the sedative too, and his tail fin flipped slightly in irritation as he leaned against the glass.

The door opened again somewhere above them, and Eron glanced over at Ket. "Just stay calm, okay? I won't let them hurt you."

Ket's ear fins moved in acknowledgement, but he stayed where he was on the bottom of the desalination tank. Styles came around the corner, Lyla following him. There were two other men with them, and Eron felt his heart leap when he recognized one of them as Marcus, Maeve's husband. He didn't say anything, just glared at Styles as the man passed him. Marcus didn't even give him a glance. Eron swallowed hard. Ket was watching the group, and the servants looked over at the mer in surprise. Eron sighed to himself. The mer were not going to be a secret much longer, that was for sure.

Lyla directed the men around a corner, and Eron heard the clink and scrape of metal before Styles suddenly reappeared, grabbing the empty tray and cup from his lap and tossing them onto a nearby surface. "Don't move," he ordered Eron before unlocking the cuffs and hauling Eron to his feet.

He let Styles pull him up. "Where are we going?" he asked, casting a worried glance at Ket.

"Back to your cell," Styles replied.

"I'd rather stay here," Eron said.

Styles shoved him along without further comment, and Eron reluctantly moved, not wanting to be dragged in a headlock or something else. He could feel Ket's eyes on him as he walked away. Styles took him back to the cell under the stairs and shoved him in. Once the door had closed and locked, he ordered Eron to stick his hands out, and Eron sighed with relief as the leather cuffs were removed. He stretched his shoulders and his neck as he turned to watch Styles head back the way he had come. He couldn't see Ket anymore, and that worried him, but there was not much he could do about that. They probably would not hurt Ket, at least; they needed him to find the other mer.

Lyla reappeared, leading the three men, and Eron watched in fascinated horror as they carried boxes that were full of the same barbed metal nets that Lyla had thrown over Ket earlier. He gripped the bars. There were several very large boxes, each filled to the top with the netting. Obviously these had not been made just now; he wondered what Lyla had originally created the nets for. Maeve had mentioned that Lyla was a scientist. Maybe the mer were not the only creatures she experimented on. Marcus gave him the smallest glance as they walked past, but Eron could not read anything in the man's dark brown eyes.

The group tramped up the stairs, over Eron's head, and then the basement door shut and locked once again. Eron sank down to sit on the slightly damp floor with a groan. What was going to happen to him? But more importantly, what would happen to Ket? He knew the mer would not want to cooperate and risk his friends, but it wasn't as if he had much choice in the matter. Lyla had made it very clear that Ket would serve a purpose, alive or dead.

Lyla came back down after a bit, ignoring Eron completely, bustling around the lab, grabbing things he couldn't see before she disappeared around the corner where he could hear her working with some sort of metal, but he couldn't see what it was. He didn't hear any noise that sounded like Ket, at least.

He thought he might have dozed off, because the cell door suddenly opened, and Styles slid a tray inside before closing and locking it again. Eron could already smell the putrid stench of fish and realized that the manservant was bringing another fish to Ket. He moved over to the tray, finding another roll, a cup of water, and some sort of soup, though no utensils for him to use. He sighed and picked up the bowl, bringing it to his lips. He heard the tank lid open, and he had just swallowed a mouthful of lukewarm broth when he heard shouting that sounded very much like Styles, a murmured answer from Lyla, and the tank lid closing again. And then Styles stalked around the corner, dripping wet from head to toe, with several fish scales sticking to his coat. Eron smirked at that as the man stormed up the stairs, reeking of fish. Whatever Ket had done, he was proud of the mer.

He picked up the roll and took a bite of it before something that was not bread touched his teeth. Eron blinked and looked down, seeing something folded into the center of the roll. The bottom of the roll was slightly indented as well, as if something had been pushed up into it. Eron ripped the bread apart with his fingers to find a small piece of paper, no bigger than his palm, folded up and stuffed inside of it. He carefully opened the paper. It was dark under the stairs, so he moved over to the bars of the cell, keeping an eye out for Lyla. There was a single hand-written line on it.

If your crew can be trusted to help you, turn bowl upside-down.

Eron blinked in surprise, then shoved the paper into his pocket. His heart leaped in his chest. Someone was trying to help him. But who would be asking him about his airship crew? He was certain that Baron Forthwell would not contact his former crew to be part of whatever whalling ships he summoned to the island. It had to be someone else. He picked up the soup bowl and looked underneath it, but there was nothing. *Turn bowl upside-down*, he mused to himself, then realized it must mean to put it upside-down on the tray.

He thought over the answer as he hurried to swallow the rest of the broth. Most whalling ship crews were pretty tight knit, as they spent so much time together, and they relied on one another for safety. But would his crew actually come to his rescue, especially against the man who literally owned their ship and was their employer? That was not just a big ask; it was a life-altering choice. Risse, of course, would want to help him, but Risse was also the newest member of the crew. Captain Byron liked him, and he would consider her his friend, but would she risk her livelihood to save him? Would Kristia be all right with that too, since Kristia would be the one to take over the ship if Captain Byron was no longer in charge? He wasn't sure he could assume anything anymore. But he definitely was not getting out of this situation by himself at this rate. He wondered how the person trying to help him would know which airship crew was his, but he had no way to communicate that either.

He quickly swallowed the rest of the bread and soup, then laid the soup bowl upside-down on the tray before pushing it back by the cell door. He shredded the paper into tiny pieces and shoved them down the drain in his cell. And then there was nothing he could do but wait. He heard Lyla working but heard nothing that sounded like Ket or the desalination tank opening. At some point, Styles and the two men returned again and headed for the area he could not see. On their way back with more boxes, of what he could not tell, one of the coils of metal on Marcus's stack fell, and he knelt to pick it up. As he did, Eron saw his eye find the upside-down soup bowl, then meet Eron's gaze for the briefest moment, so quick that Eron thought he might have imagined it. Then the servants were gone again. Eron felt a quiver of hope rise in his heart. Maybe it was Marcus and Maeve trying to help him.

He had no idea what time it was without any windows to see outside, but eventually sleep overtook him, and Eron curled up in the cell, wishing that he had Ket next to him.

When he woke up again, everything was quiet, and it was nearly pitch black in the lab. Lyla must have finished whatever she was working on. A few items on shelves and tables let off a glow or a bit of power, but the room was otherwise swathed in shadow. He debated calling out to Ket, but in the stillness of the house, he had no idea how much his voice would carry, and he did not want to bring the

Forthwells or Styles down to quiet him in the middle of the night. He took a few minutes to examine the cell and the area outside of it in case he could reach anything, but it was all in vain, so he curled back up to sleep, dreading what the morning would bring.

Chapter 10

Eron was awakened by the lights suddenly coming on and the thunder of footsteps on the stairs above him, sending him jolting upright, heart racing. Several servants hurried past him, though he could not tell if Marcus was amongst them before his view was blocked by Styles. "Up," the man ordered, and Eron got to his feet. "Hands." Eron turned and slid his hands through the bars for Styles to lock them with the leather cuffs again, before his cell door opened, and Styles began to pull him up the stairs.

Eron gave a struggle. "Where are we going? Where's Ket?"

"Keep moving," Styles grunted, and Eron found himself shoved up the stairs and into a hallway inside the manor. Then they were moving along a corridor until they stepped outside, and Eron squinted as the bright early-morning sunlight stabbed at his eyes. They were on a landing pad for the airship with the dark red balloon.

Its engines thrummed softly, and it swayed a bit in the breeze, as if it were a stabled horse that knew it was about to be set free.

The baron was already on board the airship, and he smiled coldly at Eron as Styles shoved him up the walkway and onto the deck. "Good morning, Mr. Marcel. I trust you slept well."

Eron glowered. "Where is Ket?"

"Lady Forthwell will be loading up your fish friend shortly," the baron said. "In the meantime, I wanted you to be able to see the start of this grand plan that you were able to launch for me." He waved his hand over the deck, and Eron followed his gaze to see several tiny airships on the distant horizon, making their way steadily toward the island.

"You don't have to do this," Eron said through gritted teeth. "We could find a way to work with the mer that doesn't put the whalls at risk. Something that will benefit everyone."

The baron laughed and gazed at Eron over his violet glasses. "You have a surprisingly soft heart for these animals, considering your profession, Mr. Marcel. Or maybe you just really like fucking them."

Eron glowered, knowing the baron was trying to bait him. "The mer are not animals."

Forthwell smirked. "They are not human."

"That shouldn't matter," Eron protested. "They're the closest thing to human I've seen in these waters."

"That does not necessarily make them worth saving," Forthwell said dryly. "Now, if they prove themselves to be valuable and cooperative, we can re-examine the situation. But of course, we need to understand how they live, which requires specimens."

"You would kill them just to manipulate them into helping you," Eron snarled, and the baron snorted.

"Now you're getting it, boy. That is how businesses work. Those on top control the ones on the bottom. If the ones on the bottom don't submit, they will be crushed."

Eron wanted to point out that without those 'on the bottom,' those on the top would have nothing, but he was interrupted by something being hauled aboard the ship, and he heard several familiar screeches and clicks. Currently being rolled onto the airship deck was a brass cage on a cart, and inside of the cage was Ket. It looked like a giant birdcage, but the bars were much too close together to allow Ket to slip out, even as lithe and slim as he was.

"Ah, our guest of honor," the baron said grandly, as if Ket were the Queen herself. He then turned to Eron. "Now, here is the deal, and this is the only offer you will get, so I suggest you pay attention. Once we are out to sea, your little fish friend goes in the water. It will summon its friends and a whall. The airships will catch the whall, and the sky divers will catch the mer with the nets. Should your fish try to get clever and warn them, you should make him very aware that you will be on my airship with a pistol to your head the entire time."

Eron glanced over at Styles, who pulled open his jacket to reveal a pistol tucked snugly into the pocket. Eron swallowed. "May I talk to him?" he asked, indicating the cage. The baron nodded, motioning for Styles to go with him.

Eron approached the cage. Ket was gripping the bars, curled on the bottom of it without water to support him. He looked so downcast that Eron wanted to burst into tears. Styles grabbed his shoulder and kept him a few paces from the cage.

"Are you all right?" Eron asked gently.

Ket's ear fins flicked sadly, and he motioned at Eron.

Eron nodded. "I'm all right, I promise," he said, trying to give Ket a brave smile but knowing he was failing miserably. "Once we're over the sea, the baron is going to put you in the water. He wants you to call the other mer and the whalls. Can you do that?"

Ket hesitated before his ear fins flicked again.

Eron swallowed hard. "The baron wants me to tell you that the sky divers are going to catch the mer with their nets. He says if you..." He glanced at Styles over his shoulder, who was watching him closely. "If you try to warn them, he'll kill me."

Ket let out a screech and tried to reach for him, his tail flailing madly, but he couldn't even get his hand between the tight bars of the cage. Styles' grip tightened on Eron's shoulder, enough that it drew a wince from him. The cage gave a small rock on its base as Ket slammed against it.

"It's okay! I'll be all right!" Eron said, trying to reassure him so the cage did not fall over. Ket made a clicking noise, but he went still again, though Eron could see the tremble that went through his whole body. "I will be all right. Tell the mer..." He glanced over at Styles again, then back to Ket. "Tell them not to resist the divers, all right? So they don't get hurt. I will talk to the baron and Lady Forthwell and find a way for all of you to be safe."

Ket stared at him sadly. Eron felt like his heart had just broken into a thousand clockwork pieces in his chest. "I'm so sorry," he said softly. "I should never have put you or the others in this danger, and I am so, so sorry."

Ket's eyes filled with tears, and he clicked and chirped to him. Eron smiled weakly. "I love you too, silly fish. It will be all right." The words felt bitter on his tongue. Things would not be all right. The mer were going to get hurt, the whalls were going to get killed, and it was all because of him.

Then Styles grabbed him by his shirt collar and hauled him back. Eron stumbled after him, hearing Ket screech. When he was able to look back again, Lyla was draping a large piece of canvas over the cage, as if Ket was a parrot she was trying to entice to sleep.

The four approaching airships were very close now, circling into a formation to land. Eron wanted to stay and see if he recognized any of them, but Styles dragged him to one of the storage rooms where Marcus and the others must have brought the nets the night before. He unlocked Eron's cuffs just as several other crew members entered, seeming to wait for orders. Styles jerked his head at the boxes. "Take these on deck. And you keep your mouth shut." Eron would have rather bitten off his own tongue than touch those nets, but he didn't want to risk Styles' wrath on himself or Ket, so he just picked up one of the boxes and followed the crew back out into the sunlight.

There were about a dozen assembled airship crew members from the various airships gathering on the deck, and Eron scanned them quickly. He recognized several of them, but no one he had worked with before, and no one was paying attention to him. He probably looked like any other crew member on the baron's ship.

Forthwell stepped forward, Lyla by his side. He raised his hands, and the rustle of the airship crew members went quiet, leaving only the snapping of the canvas and the thrum of the engines. "Thank you all for joining me. I am Thaddeus Forthwell, the owner of

Wind and Sea Enterprises. I have called you here today because we have a great new opportunity in the world of deep-sea exploration. This," he gestured to the covered cage. The canvas was suddenly unceremoniously yanked off by Lyla, and a collective gasp went up from the crew as Ket blinked in the sudden light, still curled in the bottom of the cage. "Is a newly discovered creature, currently called a mer. I have come to learn that there are more of them in the sea, and that they are in communication not only with each other, but also with the whalls."

Another rumble rippled through the crowd. Eron couldn't blame them. He probably would have reacted the same way if he had been seeing a mer for the first time and finding out their connection to the whalls.

The baron smiled coldly. "These creatures can not only summon the whalls and their fellow mer, but I have also learned that the mer can find pearls." He held up the two pink pearls Ket had given him the other night, and Eron clenched his jaw. Several of the crew members rustled excitedly. The prospect of getting more treasures, especially pearls, from the sea would appeal to any whall hunter.

Forthwell brushed his hand over his muttonchops. "I have summoned you here as my best of the best crews. We are going to go out to sea, where the creature will summon more mer and whalls. I want your gunners prepared to fire on any whalls, but the priority is the mer." The baron gestured to the boxes Eron and the others held. "These nets have been specially prepared. I want your best sky divers in the water, ready to catch them. As an incentive," the baron added, glancing over the assembled crews. "For every live mer caught, that crew will get a thousand Struck to share. Four hundred for every dead one."

Eron's stomach dropped into his boots as a cheer went up from the assembled hunters. Knowing the mer could be dead or injured and the crew would still get their bounty would guarantee that the sky divers would not be overly careful with the mer. His arms wobbled, and he landed on his knee with his box, inhaling sharply. Styles watched him, but the baron barely gave him a glance. He gestured at the crew holding the nets to bring them to the assembled divers. Eron stayed where he was. Someone scooped up the box of nets from in front of him, but he was shaking too hard to even lift his head.

The assembled divers began to talk excitedly as they exited back to their own airships, and Eron watched any of them for signs of concern or that they might be willing to help him, but no one was paying attention to him. He gritted his teeth as Styles grabbed his wrists and locked them behind him with the leather cuffs again. Ket was gripping the bars of the cage, and even across the deck, Eron could see him trembling too.

The airship engines began to thrum louder, and Eron felt the ballasts be released, leaving the ship hovering with nothing tethering her to the ground. Then there was a loud whoosh of steam, and the airship began to rise and drift over the edge of the landing pad. Eron glanced down, watching the cliffs of the islands rapidly fall away underneath them. Normally he enjoyed this part of an airship departure, but as they left solid ground behind, his heart sank lower and lower. There was only air around them, and the sea below them.

The other airships began to lift off and follow after them in careful formation so as not to be in the way of steam blasts or wind currents of the other ships. Eron could tell that all of their captains were skilled whall hunters and excellent pilots, which just made his anxiety worse. If they were half as good as the crew and captain of the SERENITY, their dive teams would be excellent.

Lyla seemed to be giving instructions to the captain at the helm of their elaborate airship where to go, though Eron could not hear what she said. He watched the waves move beneath them, the island getting smaller and smaller behind them. Port Ceyran was on their starboard side, and they seemed to be flying almost parallel to it. Lyla came down from the helm and crossed the deck, stopping briefly to talk to her father, and they shared a moment of cold laughter that sent chills over Eron even without hearing their words.

Lyla moved to a control panel on the starboard side toward the bow of the airship, pulling a lever on it to lower a winch toward the deck. Eron followed its trail up and realized with another jolt to his stomach that the winch was on a crane arm track that could swing out over the port side of the airship. He had a horrible image of Ket dangling hundreds of feet in the air. Several crew members stepped forward, surrounding the cage, and Eron heard Ket give a frightened hiss. A few of the crew backed up a step, but Lyla laughed. "It won't hurt you. It has no claws either." Eron realized glumly that Lyla was right. The bars were too close together for Ket to get his head through to bite anyone, and even if he could manage to slip his arm through, the most he could do would be to grab someone. But the mer did not have unusual strength, and between the lack of fresh food and his injuries, he doubted Ket had much energy to do anything, even if he did latch onto someone.

While the crew worked to secure the cage to the winch, Ket curled into a tight ball in the bottom, watching the whole proceeding with terrified, amber eyes. The wind whipped past them as the airship moved, and Eron was momentarily glad Ket was curled where he could not easily see the open air around them. Flying through the air was hard enough for humans who were used to it; for a mer who had lived underwater all of his life, he was sure it would be absolutely terrifying. He caught glimpses of Ket as the crew moved around and tried to send him reassurance with his eyes, but his own heart was pounding so much, he wouldn't have been surprised if Ket could hear it all the way across the open deck.

The airship continued to travel until Port Ceyran was only a speck on the horizon and the island was no longer visible. Lyla had a pair of bi-oculars to her eyes and appeared to be studying the water. Eron glanced over the railing as best he could from where he and Styles stood. What she was looking for, he was unsure, but she seemed satisfied by whatever she saw, and the airship began to slow. Lyla moved back over to the control panel and pulled the lever. The winch began to raise, and the cable holding the cage pulled taut. The cage rocked for a moment, and then began to swing a little as it lifted off the deck entirely.

Eron glowered at Lyla. "If you drop that cage in the water from this height, it will kill him."

"I am not a fool, Mr. Marcel," Lyla said, rolling her eyes as she pulled down her goggles.

Eron started toward the cage. Styles yanked him back by his collar, and Eron choked. "My hands are tied," he pointed out. "I just want to make sure he's all right."

"You've had your time with the creature," Forthwell replied with a sneer.

Eron glowered. "He has a name."

The baron waved his hand, his gold rings catching the light from the sun that was starting to crest the sky. "You best mind yourself, Mr. Marcel, or you'll go into the water with him, and I have yet to see any gills on you." Eron went cold. If he went into the water with his arms locked behind him, he would have very little chance of being able to get to the surface again.

"Descending," the captain called, and there was a loud whoosh of steam as the airship slowly began to lower. Eron felt the familiar rise of his stomach. He could tell Ket felt it too, because the mer suddenly looked incredibly nauseous. Eron had no idea if Ket could throw up, but if he could, he hoped the mer would do so all over Lyla.

Lyla adjusted something on the control panel, and the cable holding the cage off the deck lifted it a little higher. Ket let out a screech, wrapping his fingers around the bars tightly, like he expected the bottom to fall out from under him. Eron surged toward him, but an elbow slammed into his back, and he stumbled forward, twisting just enough to land painfully on his shoulder rather than his face. He heard the click of a pistol being cocked, and he froze.

"Get to your knees, but no further," Forthwell said calmly. Eron turned to look at Ket, who was staring at him in wide-eyed panic. He kept eye contact with the mer as he rolled onto his stomach and slowly pushed himself up to kneeling on the deck. Something brushed the back of his head, and he flinched away from it, knowing it was the barrel of a gun.

The crane arm began to swing, moving the cage across the deck and over the railing, out into the open air. Ket let out a screech as the cage swung back and forth wildly like a pendulum, and Eron imagined the winch breaking and the cage plummeting. "Ket, stay still, please!" Ket whined softly but just clung to the bars. After a few moments of swaying, the cage eventually settled into a small rocking motion.

And then the cage began to lower, the cable slowly unspooling with a clockwork sound. Ket let out a squeak, turning his eyes toward Eron. "It's okay," Eron tried to soothe him, in spite of the pistol pressed lightly against his temple.

The cage disappeared from view, and after another moment, Eron heard it touch the water and submerge. His lungs suddenly felt too tight, as if he were the one plunging into the sea. The winch kept going for what he guessed must have been a couple dozen more feet before it stopped. Ket was all alone under the water in that cage, and if anything went wrong, there was nowhere for him to go. But now all they could do was wait. He had no idea how far out the nearest whall or group of mer would be, but he hoped that Ket would be able to make himself heard underwater for a great distance for just such a reason.

Every minute that ticked by felt like an eternity. Eron was trying hard not to get twitchy, as he had no idea what might set off Styles or the baron, but if he could have, he would have leaped into the water to go search for Ket himself. Around him, the other airships hovered, and Eron could see their gunners prepped on the decks and sky divers ready to go into the water in their whall hide suits, the barbed nets slung over shoulders or in the retrieval boats.

The only person on their airship who seemed to be moving much at all was Lyla. She drifted to the railings to look over the water, disappeared into the hold below to check on things that Eron didn't want to think about, then would reappear and check the winch cable and control box. Around and around she went, until Eron wanted to scream at her to just stop fucking moving, but he didn't dare say a word with Styles and Baron Forthwell so close to him.

Eventually food was served, and Styles unlocked Eron's hands just long enough for him to swallow some water and shove a hasty meal into his mouth. He wondered if Ket had gotten any breakfast, or if he was able to catch any fish through the bars of the cage.

The sun moved across the sky; Eron was sure several hours had gone by, hours full of nothing but waiting. He was sweating even in his lighter clothing. The baron had retreated into the deck cabin and was sipping from a crystal glass of dark liquor, his dark eyebrows furrowed in annoyance. Eron couldn't help but smirk. The baron was used to his commands being obeyed immediately, not sitting around waiting for prey to appear. That was for the people on the bottom, like him, to do. Styles had at least moved into some shade with him, though he did not allow Eron to sit, and Eron tried hard not to shift from foot to foot. Between the heat and his anxiety, he felt like a harpoon launcher pulled tight, just waiting to be released.

The baron finally came out of his cabin and crossed over to Eron. "What is taking your fish so long?"

Eron shrugged. "I don't know. I can't see him any more than you can."

"Your impertinence is not helpful, boy."

"I've done what I can do," Eron shot back, watching Forthwell's face turn bright red. "I'm not a mer or a whall."

Styles grabbed him by the back of his neck and suddenly connected his foot with the back of Eron's knee. Eron landed on the deck with a gasp of pain, the two bigger men gazing down at him. At least their looming forms blocked out the sunlight.

"Perhaps your fish needs some motivation," the baron said, tipping Eron's chin up with his hand. "How long can you hold your breath, Mr. Marcel?"

Eron knew that was not a genuine question, and his stomach flip-flopped inside of him. "It's the ocean," he said through clenched teeth. "It doesn't obey your money or your threats."

The baron raised his fist, and Eron prepared himself to be struck in the face when a shout came over the water. "Whall off the port side!"

Eron sucked in a breath as Styles hauled him up, and the baron, Lyla, and the crew hurried to the edge of the airship to look. Eron could just see a dark shape moving under the water, coming in surprisingly fast for a whall. He swallowed hard as he heard various shouts from the airships around them as the gunners prepared to launch harpoons, and all he could do was hope that Ket had communicated the danger to the incoming whall.

And then everything went shockingly quiet. Eron could hear his own blood racing in his ears even over the roar of the waves and the hum of all of the airship engines. The dark form that had been careening toward the airships was suddenly gone. He could see gunners and crew scanning the water's surface, looking for any sign of the whall, but the sea was unperturbed.

Eron saw the winch line move a split second before the entire airship jerked, and he grabbed onto the first piece of ship that he could that was bolted down. The airship was suddenly pulled violently sideways, pivoting in the air until it was being dragged by the winch line, away from the other airships. Crew members screamed and were flung about the deck. Next to him, Styles stumbled, and Eron took his chance, slamming his shoulder as hard as he could into the man. The gun hit the deck with a clatter as Styles stumbled backward, and he pitched over the side of the deck with a shout that was lost in the roar of the wind. Eron slid across the deck on his backside and caught himself against the deck railing, gripping it behind him with his bound hands.

The airship charged on for several more long moments before the line went slack, and Eron braced himself as the airship kept going but the weight pulling it did not, and everything and everyone on the deck slid across it to the other side. Several crew members went over the side, and Eron heard them hit the water with a loud splash. The airship pivoted again against the winch rope.

Eron struggled to his feet, looking around for the dropped pistol, but it had vanished in the chaos. He looked back to see the four other airships far away now, barely more than white specks on the horizon. He wasn't sure if they would come after the baron's airship but was not able to give it much thought as the ship continued to lazily spin in the air, several crew members who had been tossed around scrambling to grab the helm's wheel.

Eron suddenly heard the familiar rumble of another airship engine. Something blocked out the sun as the baron's airship finally stopped its lazy pirouetting, and the SERENITY slowed and hovered a few yards away. Eron felt a moment of pride swell in his chest as he caught sight of it. He scanned the deck and saw many familiar faces, but three of them were missing. He did not see Risse, Kristia, or Isaiah anywhere.

Captain Lavinia Byron appeared at the railing of the deck, her dark hair up in a bun under her top hat, gazing across at the baron. Forthwell stared at her, then glanced over at the side of the ship where SERENITY was painted in brilliant crimson letters. "Ah, Captain Byron," he said pleasantly, as if the entire moment had been planned.

"Your lordship," Lavinia said, gazing across at him.

"I did not invite you and your crew to this gathering."

"No, you didn't," she agreed, propping one foot up on the railing. "But whalling crews don't leave one of their own behind, and you have one of mine."

The baron turned to peg Eron with a glower. "This troublemaker? You want him back?"

"I do," Lavinia said firmly.

"Well, you can have him," Forthwell said unconcernedly. "I will send him aboard right now."

"I'm not leaving without Ket," Eron said, making sure his voice was loud enough for everyone aboard both airships to hear.

The baron sneered. "This is your one chance to go free, Mr. Marcel."

"Give Ket to me, and I will."

The baron laughed loudly, his voice echoing off the snapping canvas of both airships. "That creature is mine." He turned back to Captain Byron again. "You would throw away your career, your ship, and your crew's means of living for one ungrateful sky diver?"

"No," Lavinia said, and Eron swallowed hard. "But I would give all of that up for a friend in danger. So I say to you again, your lordship, free Eron and the creature he has with him. He has committed no crime. You cannot keep him prisoner."

Forthwell laughed at that. "He is under my employ, and, as far as the world knows, he is dead."

"My crew knows otherwise," Lavinia said.

"And I resigned as a whall hunter," Eron added. "I no longer work for you."

"Ah, that settles it then," Lavinia replied. "We will return Mr. Marcel to his home for his own safety. And his creature, as I am sure he has not been compensated for it."

The baron laughed darkly. "I am your employer, and I give the orders, Captain. Stand down, or you and your crew will be arrested for piracy."

Captain Byron pursed her lips. "Surely we can discuss this in a civilized manner, your lordship. You seem to be a reasonable man of business."

Eron had to stop a snort of laughter. While Lavinia's words sounded genuine, he had known her long enough to be able to hear the underlying sarcasm in her tone.

"I am indeed," the baron said. "I am surprised at you, Captain, after all your years of service, you would throw away a career for a single whall hunter."

"I did not get to where I am by leaving my crew behind," Lavinia said with a bright smile. "So, if you please-"

A sudden rattling noise filled the air, and Eron's heart nearly stopped as he realized it was the sound of a gatling gun. He ducked without even knowing where the sound was coming from, but he heard the sound of canvas ripping and realized with horror that it came from the SERENITY's balloon that kept the ship aloft. The crew on board the SERENITY all ducked as well, bullets peppering the side of the airship. Several of the balloon's mooring lines snapped, and the airship pitched to the side, steam starting to spew from several of the holes in the hold where the water tanks were. Eron's throat dropped into his stomach as the SERENITY began to lose pressure and slowly descended toward the water, which at least was not very far.

Someone stepped up next to him, and Eron almost leaped out of his skin as Laurisse clapped a hand to his shoulder. "Hey."

"Fucking hell!" Eron gasped, turning to his friend who had his goggles pulled down over his eyes and was wearing his whall-skin diving gear. "Risse?"

"Yeah, I got you, man," Risse said, reaching behind Eron and unlatching the clasp that held Eron's wrists together. Eron turned just in time to see Isaiah and Kristia, also in diving gear, point pistols at the airship crew.

"Everyone over here," Kristia said, motioning with her gun barrel toward the cabin at the bow of the ship. The crew members on Forthwell's ship were not fighters or even whall hunters; they were a private airship crew, with no weapons and no fighting experience. They all complied hastily, hands raised. Kristia kept the pistol pointed at them, motioning toward the cabin. "All of you, inside," she said in a voice that boded no discussion.

Isaiah ushered everyone inside the cabin before closing the door and jamming it with a piece of metal so the door would not open.

Eron nearly collapsed, grabbing Risse's shoulder to steady himself. "God... damn..." he breathed. "Where the hell did you come from?"

Risse grinned, gesturing behind them to the port side where the winch still dangled the cable into the water. "Swam under the ship once the whall stopped pulling you, and then I used this," he motioned to something on his hip that looked like a pneumatic pistol but had a grappling hook at the end of it, "to get us up to the deck while the Captain distracted everyone."

That answered most of the questions that Eron had, but his eyes landed on the crane arm still stretched over the water. "Oh god, did you see if the cage was still attached to the cable while you were down there?"

Risse shook his head. "Sorry, man, we weren't down that low. The cable is still taut though, so whatever's down there is probably still there."

"We need to get it out of the water!" Eron said, pointing to the control panel.

"Got it," Risse said and sprinted over to the box.

Kristia appeared by Eron's side, in the middle of sliding off her diving gear. "All right, Eron?"

"Yeah," Eron replied, giving her a bright smile. "Thank you."

The winch began to grind upward, and Isaiah came over to give Eron's shoulder a squeeze. "Glad to see you still alive, Marcel."

"Same to you, Cam," Eron replied. "You all did not have to risk your lives and your jobs like this."

Kristia rolled her eyes behind her goggles. "You think we were going to let some rich bastard keep you prisoner?"

"Who contacted you?" Eron asked in surprise.

"Someone named Maeve," Kristia said. "She contacted her son in Port Ceyran, who delivered a message to Captain Byron."

Eron made a mental note to thank Maeve and Marcus profusely for their help. Most likely their careers as servants for Baron Forthwell were over too, so he would have to make sure they were cared for. He was distracted from this line of thought by hearing something break the surface of the water, and he dashed to the railing. He looked down and saw that the cage was still attached, and, in the bottom of it, clinging to the bars as water poured between them, was Ket. Eron let out a sharp breath. "Ket!" he called. The mer looked up, and even from their distance apart, Eron could see Ket stare at him and then smile. "Hold on, we'll get you up."

The winch suddenly juttered to a halt, and Risse looked up at the crane arm. "Fuck," he groaned. "The tie line is snagged around it."

Kristia glanced up at the damaged rope that had wrapped itself around the winch. "I'm on it!" She shoved her goggles down over her eyes, and suddenly she was climbing the rope line with the grace and speed of a monkey even as the wind whipped around her. She pried at the jammed rope with her gloved hands, trying to loosen where it had caught around the arm and kept the winch from winding further. He glanced down at Ket, who was staring at Kristia with wide, scared eyes, water still streaming off him and from the cage.

He almost missed it over the sounds of the wind and the ocean, but somewhere Eron registered a thump and something heavy hitting the deck. He turned to see Isaiah slumped on the stairs leading up to the helm, blood oozing down his face from a cut across his temple. Someone grabbed the airship's controls; it was Lyla. She shoved a lever, and the airship gave a sudden jerk, steam hissing loudly, canvas snapping. The vessel suddenly began to ascend rapidly. Eron watched in horror as the jolt made Kristia lose her balance around the winch. But she had locked her ankles together underneath her and suddenly hung upside-down from the arm like a bespectacled bat. He reached a hand toward her, though he was hopelessly too far to grab her.

"Go, I got Kris!" Risse shouted at him, and Eron sprinted for the stairs. He leaped over Isaiah, not having the time to check if the man was all right, before he lunged at Lyla. She leaped backward, away from the wheel, and the airship stalled to a halt and leveled out again. He grabbed her wrists, and she kicked fiercely at him. Eron avoided it, but they scuffled and went tumbling down the stairs, narrowly missing Isaiah, both of them hitting the deck with a thump that reverberated off the canvas. Eron quickly rolled onto his side and pushed himself up, though everything hurt, and he felt like he had bruised at least a few ribs in the fall. Lyla was on the deck, looking dazed, blood covering her face from a cut somewhere.

"Eron!" Risse called and slid the leather cuffs across the deck to him. Eron snatched them up and quickly locked Lyla's hands together around the railing. He turned again to see Kristia was back on top of the crane arm, working at the rope that was still jamming the winch. Eron felt his heart in his throat. If the crane broke now, Ket was still locked in the cage and wouldn't be able to get out. From this height, the cage would be smashed if it fell and hit the water. Eron wanted to call out to Ket, to reassure him that it would be all right, but he didn't want to distract Kristia.

The rope came free with a sudden snap, and the winch whined and began to pull the cage up again. Kristia leaped to her feet and balanced along the arm before hopping back onto the deck of the airship. Eron had never considered himself a hugger, but he could not stop himself from wrapping his arms tightly around her. "You're all right!"

"Of course, I am," Kristia said, her face mushed against Eron's chest. "This is very awkward."

"Sorry," Eron said, letting her go.

Kristia pushed her goggles up to look at him with a bright grin as the winch continued to wind. "I appreciate the sentiment, Marcel. Come on, help me get the cage in."

The arm was swinging now, Ket clinging to the bars again as he stared at Eron. The cage bumped lightly over the railing of the airship, and Risse pulled another lever to lower it carefully to the ground. Ket whined and was scrambling against the bars. Eron pressed his hand flat against the damp metal. "Hold on, we're getting you out," he soothed. Risse came over with a key and inserted it into the lock. It clicked, and he gave it a pull open.

Ket nearly launched himself into Eron's arms. Eron caught him, barely managing to keep Ket against him with the dampness of his scales, Ket pressing his nose to Eron's eagerly, his arms going around Eron's neck so tight that he almost couldn't breathe, but he didn't care. "I've got you," he whispered, and Ket's ear fin flicked. "You're going to be all right."

Kristia and Risse were both staring at Ket, and Eron realized that they had never seen the mer before. He flushed and turned to them. "Um, this is Ket. He rescued me when we capsized last week. He's a mer."

"A what?" Kristia asked.

"A mer," Eron repeated.

"I have no idea what that is, but if he saved you, he's all right in my book," Kristia said. "You all right, Ket?"

Ket turned to stared at her curiously before smiling and flicking his ear fins. Eron laughed. "That means yes."

Kristia grinned and held out her hand to Ket. "Kristia Llewellyn."

Ket stared at the hand for a moment before turning to Eron in confusion. Eron laughed and took Kristia's hand in a handshake. "This is how humans say hello."

Ket beamed and took Kristia's hand in his, giving it an enthusiastic shake. Kristia laughed. "You're cute. I can see why Eron likes you."

Eron felt his cheeks heat bright red. "Can we not talk about that right now?"

Kristia nodded. "I'm going to check on Cam."

She hurried across the deck toward Isaiah, and Eron turned to Risse, who was still staring at Ket in surprise. "This is Laurisse, my best friend," he said. Ket blinked, then held out his hand to Risse, who took it and gave it an awkward shake.

"Nice to meet you," Risse said. Eron could already see that Risse had a million questions about Ket, and all he could do was be glad that both Ket and Risse were alive. Ket gave a few bright clicks in return, making Risse grin.

A gunshot rang out, echoing sharply over the open deck and the canvas. Eron heard something whistle past him, heat suddenly burning across his left ear, and he realized with a start that the bullet had grazed him. He turned to see Baron Forthwell standing across the deck, Styles' pistol in his hand, pointed directly at him. His breath caught, and all he could think was he needed to dodge but there was nowhere to go.

"Hold on!" Kristia yelled, diving for the helm, and then the entire airship suddenly began to tip toward the port side. The baron shifted his feet, but the airship kept listing, and he lost his footing, landing hard and starting to slide down the deck. The gun slid faster, through the railing and out into the open air. The baron kept coming, and Eron knew he was not going to be able to get out of the way. Risse had his hand wrapped around one of the leather straps bolted along the railing, and Eron found the one next to him and shoved Ket's hand onto it, just as Forthwell's bulk collided with him. The jolt sent them both tumbling, hitting the railing and bouncing off and over it.

Eron clamped onto the only thing his scrambling hands could find: one of the many ropes that lined the hull of the ship. His fingers closed around it, jerking his fall to a stop. He nearly lost his grip on the rope as it slid through his hands, burning his fingers and the skin of his palms. His shout of pain was lost to the wind. What was not was the scream that was wrenched from his throat as Forthwell grasped him by the ankle and caused Eron to slide down the rope, slicing into his already burned skin. His fingers strained to hold on, the wind whipping around him, threatening to dislodge him from his precarious position.

Forthwell's grip on Eron's leg was like an anchor pulling him down. His hands shrieked in pain as he clung to the rope, his shoulders and hip wrenching as Forthwell dug his fingers into Eron's leg, the sharp agony of his bruised ribs making his vision go gray for a moment. He started to kick at the man, but the empty air around them made him stall his movements. He couldn't just let the baron fall, no matter how much he wanted to. A fall from this distance would kill him. But his own body was stretching to its limit, and the fire in his hands and torso was only getting worse.

The airship slowly righted itself again, and Eron could feel every agonizing second in his body as he desperately clung to the single rope that was keeping him and the baron aloft. Forthwell's hands scrabbled at Eron's leg, trying to hook into the waist of his pants to get more leverage.

Risse and Isaiah appeared at the edge of the railing, reaching out desperate arms down to him, but they were still not quite close enough to grab him. One of his hands slipped again, and Eron screamed at the pain, the baron jerking his leg sharply as he clung to him. He looked up again to see Ket suddenly appear between Risse and Isaiah, staring at him with wide eyes. He felt his grip loosen and slide, and tears stung his eyes. At least Ket would be the last thing he saw before he fell.

With a feral snarl, Ket suddenly leaped over the side of the railing, his scaly tail a blur of blue past Eron. Ket caught himself on Forthwell's jacket and sank his sharp teeth into the arm holding Eron's ankle. The baron let out a yell of pain and lost his grip. The weight was suddenly gone from Eron, but he felt his heart drop in horror as Ket plummeted downward toward the water, after the baron's tumbling form. He screamed and reached for Ket, even though the mer was hopelessly out of his grasp already. He started to let go of the airship rope, but suddenly Risse and Isaiah had grabbed his wrists. They hauled him physically up over the ledge, even as Eron heard himself yelling, as if from a great distance. He was on his feet and back at the railing before they had even let go of him, staring down at the churning surface of the sea. There was a large splash ring forming from where something heavy had hit the water, but neither the baron nor Ket was visible.

Eron felt the sob catch in his throat, and his knees gave out as he leaned against the railing, shaking. Ket was gone; he had saved Eron, only to be lost to him forever.

Arms went around him, holding him tightly, and he wasn't sure who he leaned against as his body wracked itself with sobs. His hands came up to grip someone's elbow, and he felt the shock of pain go through them again, but it felt so distant as the mind-numbing tears found their way down his cheeks.

The warm embrace held him for a long minute until the airship jolted, landing on the sea with a thunk of wood against water. He had been crying so hard he had not even noticed their descent. Everything around him felt like ice, numbing his body until he couldn't feel anything anymore except for the pain in his heart that spilled down his face. He had tried so hard to save Ket, and in the end, it had been for nothing.

There was a splash nearby. Someone let go of Eron and moved away, and he curled tighter against Isaiah's chest.

"Eron." Something in Risse's voice made him lift his head. He was standing by the railing, gazing down. Eron struggled to his feet, his limbs sluggish, Isaiah supporting him most of the way up. He stumbled to the railing, and his breath left him in a startled gasp.

The SERENITY's retrieval boat bobbed in the water, with Captain Byron and the rest of the crew. Next to the boat, two heads with ear fins peeked out of the water. Two mer, one of whom he recognized as the dark-haired one they had traveled with, had risen out of the water, something cradled in their arms. It was Ket. His eyes were closed, but Eron could see the barely-there rise and fall of the young mer's chest. The dark-haired mer lifted Ket all the way out of the water, and Eron stifled a sob.

"Ket," he moaned softly, reaching for him, though he was hopelessly too far up on the deck. Isaiah passed him into Kristia's arms before moving over to lower the mooring lines down to the retrieval boat. The SERENITY crew attached the cables as Captain Byron offered her hands to the two mer. They looked surprised but let her help them into the small craft, laying Ket gently down in it, until the boat was pulled onto the airship. The crew hurried off of the retrieval boat, and then Risse and Kristia held out their hands to help the two mer out. The dark-haired one grasped Risse's hand, and for just a brief moment, their eyes locked, and they stared at one another. Eron looked down, flushing at the unexpected connection, gazing instead at the curled form they still held. He moved over to them, and the mer deposited Ket gently into his arms. He cuddled him close, heedless of the water that soaked him and the salt that stung his palms like hellfire. Ket's beautiful fin at the end of his tail was ragged on one side, and the other side of it was gone, completely ripped off. He brushed a few strands of Ket's hair off the pale forehead as he held him close to his chest. "Will he live?"

The dark-haired mer's ear fins quivered in the familiar gesture that Eron knew meant 'yes.' He let out another breath, letting the tears fall now. "Thank you," he said. The mer gave his ear fins another acknowledging flick.

Risse lifted the end of Ket's tail, studying the ruined fin. Eron turned to him as he took Ket's hand and gave the back of it a kiss. "What do you think?"

Risse was silent for a moment, moving a few of the ruined fin pieces back and forth, before he said, "It might take some time, but I think I can help him."

"Please," Eron moaned, and Risse gave him a gentle smile.

"I will. You just take care of him until then."

Ket suddenly stirred, blinking golden eyes before turning them up to Eron. Eron sucked in a breath, leaning down to press their noses together. "Ket," he breathed. Ket seemed a bit dazed, gazing up at Eron, then at the two mer sitting on the deck nearby. The dark-haired mer said something to Ket in their clicking language, and Ket responded with a few clicks of his own that sounded tired but appreciative before his eyes turned up to Eron again.

Eron held the mer against his chest, heedless of the damp, and kissed his hair again. "Silly fish. You scared me so bad."

Ket let out a few clicks that sounded like an apology and wrapped his arms around Eron tightly, leaning up to press his lips enthusiastically to Eron's. Then he let out a soft squeak, pulling back and shifting his tail. He looked down at it in dismay, giving the ruined fin a cautious flick. His arms tightened around Eron. "Risse is going to fix you," Eron soothed, stroking Ket's hair behind his ear fin. "It will be all right."

Ket looked up at Risse, who smiled at him, before he glanced over at the other two mer, and a short conversation was exchanged between them. Ket nestled back against Eron's chest with a soft, contented sound almost like a purr, and Eron stroked his hair again. "Does it hurt?"

Ket shook his head, closing his eyes.

"Oh damn, has anyone seen that blond-haired bitch?" Kristia suddenly asked. Eron turned to look where he had locked Lyla to the stairs, but now only the cuffs remained, somehow undone, and Lady Forthwell was nowhere to be seen.

Captain Byron sighed, glancing around. "Let the crew out, they won't hurt us. We need to get a call in to the port authorities."

Eron's head shot up, and he clutched Ket to his chest. "The other whalling ships. They're going after the mer. We need to stop them."

"We'll handle it," Kristia said. "You just take care of your boy."

Eron flushed, and Kristia gave him a wink before turning to Captain Byron. Ket curled close to Eron, sighing softly. Eron ran his hand through Ket's damp hair. "Are you really all right, silly fish?"

Ket's ear fins flicked, and he leaned up to press his nose to Eron's. Eron smiled weakly. "I'm so sorry you and the other mer were put in danger because of me."

Ket let out a few tired-sounding clicks, hugging Eron tightly. Risse looked up from where he was still examining Ket's ruined tail. "Is that how they communicate?" Eron nodded. Risse hummed thoughtfully. "Might take me a while, but I think I could figure out how their language works."

Ket perked up a bit, and Eron laughed. "Would you like to help Risse with that?"

Ket's ear fins flickered wildly. "I can't wait to learn more," Eron said, stroking a hand lovingly over Ket's scaly hip. "At least I already know the most important phrase." And he kissed Ket firmly as the sun began its downward descent from the sky into the edge of the shimmering sea.

Epilogue

ERON SANG SOFTLY TO himself as he cut up pieces of apple. Ket was being extraordinarily patient with Risse, who was fitting him with pieces for his new tail fin, so he had made sure to pick up extra apples in port today. It had taken a few tries to find something that was flexible and responsive enough to Ket's movements without being too heavy, but Risse was confident that he was on the right track, each subsequent piece better than the last. Luckily, Ket had not had to do much swimming in the last few weeks.

Eron had found out from Captain Byron and the port authorities that not a single mer had been captured by the whalling crews. Ket had warned them to stay deep, where divers couldn't go, until the whall had returned for them.

Both Lyla and Styles had been found alive in a lifeboat a few hours later, along with several divers and crew members who had ended up in the water. Lyla and Styles had returned to the Forthwell home; Eron suspected the port authorities had been paid off to ignore any of Eron's complaints about kidnapping. Enough of Baron Forthwell had been found to confirm that he was dead, which satisfied Eron in that respect. Both the SERENITY and the baron's airship had been towed into Port Ceyran.

The next day, Ket had said something to his fellow mer when they visited him, and they had disappeared into the water with surprising enthusiasm. The dark-haired mer, whom Eron had eventually figured out was called Tath, had arrived at the SERENITY a day later with a bag full of pearls of all shapes, sizes, and colors, so many that Eron almost refused the entire thing on principle. The single sack of pearls was worth millions of Struck. A handful of them alone would have provided enough for him to live on for the rest of his life. But he had a lot of people to thank for helping him, so he finally accepted it, determined to put all of it to good use.

The pearls were sold, and the money parsed out. Captain Byron used her share to buy the SERENITY from Wind and Sea Enterprises, which was more than happy for the flow of Struck since the baron had disappeared. She fixed it up, and she and Kristia, along with most of the crew, became an airship for hire, which especially became necessary when word got out about the mer who lived in the sea, and scientists wanted to study them. From a respectful distance, of course, Captain Byron always informed them, and only with the mers' permission.

Eron had Marcus and Maeve brought to the mainland and gave them shares of the Struck, as well as a share for their son, Nelson. He had never been so grateful for the help of strangers before, and he had cried when he had seen Maeve for the first time since his imprisonment, holding her tight, and she stroked his hair and reassured him that all was well. His sister, Emma, had been overjoyed that he was still alive after the whalling accident, and Eron promised her that she and Michael and Faith could meet Ket once the mer was feeling better.

Eron left his apartment on the mainland and purchased an airship for himself, and Risse joined him. They stayed docked in the shallows not far off from Port Ceyran, close enough to come to the port any time they needed but in water shallow enough that the mer were safe from predators. There was a large workshop for Risse, and Eron had several spots modified so that the mer could safely come and go as they pleased through hatches in the hull. Tath came frequently to visit Risse, which Ket actually seemed delighted about.

Ket had spent most of the last few weeks in a comfortable bed on Eron's new ship, Eron waiting on him hand and tail when he needed something. He had some residual pain now from his fin injury, but it seemed tolerable, and Eron was more than happy to distract Ket with apples and kisses whenever Ket demanded either from him. And Ket demanded. Risse seemed to find it hilarious how much Eron let Ket boss him around, but Eron didn't care. He had Ket, and they were safe together.

"How does that feel?" Risse asked, tightening the last strap in place. Ket gave his tail a flick, then beamed at Risse. "Want to give it a try?"

Ket slid off the bed and over to one of the hatches Eron had made that specifically let Ket into their shared rooms. He pulled open the hatch and slipped down into the water, disappearing from view.

Eron sat down at the table, and Risse came to join him, wiping his hands on a cloth as he did before taking one of the apple slices for himself. "I got an invitation," he said casually, tossing back his hair.

"Yeah?" Eron asked, picking up his cup of tea.

"To work with some of the Queen's scientists."

Eron choked, snatching up his napkin to cough into it until he had cleared the tea from his lungs. "You're serious?" he asked in surprise. Risse grinned and nodded. "To study the mer?"

"Yeah," Risse said. "The Queen wants to know how they are being affected by whall hunting and what we can do. I think hunting whalls will become illegal very soon."

"I really hope so," Eron said, clearing his throat and taking another careful sip of tea. "That's incredible!"

"I'm looking forward to it," Risse said with a chuckle.

"Will you meet the Queen?"

"Maybe."

Eron immediately started making plans in his head to have a beautiful pearl necklace created to present to her when whall hunting was outlawed.

Risse stretched lazily. "It's been a long day. You going to wait for Ket?"

Eron nodded. "Yeah. Go rest, you'll need your beauty sleep for the Queen."

Risse smirked. "Pretty sure I have that covered," he said, tossing back his hair again before getting up from his chair and heading out and down the hall toward his rooms.

Eron sat, fiddling with his cup of tea as he waited for Ket to return. It had only been a few weeks, but so much had happened in that time. His whole world had been turned upside-down because of one creature who dared to save him when he would otherwise have died.

The sun had started to sink before Ket reappeared, sliding up through the hatch and into the living space. "Hey," Eron said. "You were gone a long time. Your tail must feel pretty good then?"

Ket clicked eagerly and stretched it out, giving it a playful wiggle, several droplets spattering Eron as he did. Eron laughed and moved over to scoop him up and spin with him, water flying around the room, and Ket giggled. He pressed his nose to Eron's, then pulled back to look at him. He opened his hand and held it up for Eron to see. In his palm were two pearls. They shimmered with an opalescent blue that caught the light and gleamed every color of the rainbow. Eron gasped. "Ket..."

Ket smiled and set one into Eron's hand. Eron closed his fingers around the pearl. "I don't know what to say. Thank you."

Ket clicked and chirped, leaning up to press their lips together. Eron held him tightly, feeling the warm dampness of Ket's body against his and knowing he never wanted to be without that feeling again. "I love you too, silly fish."

About the Author

Kit Barrie (she/her) was raised by pirates in a traveling carnival where she learned how to fly and to weave fantasy into reality. She identifies as chaotic bisexual, with good intentions and questionable methods. She lives in an utterly unfantastical state in the Midwestern United States with her very supportive spouse (VSS) and at least 4 food goblins who might just be cats gobblin' food.

Please visit www.kitbarrie.com or scan the QR code below for more information on Kit and her other available titles.

www.ingramcontent.com/pod-product-compliance
Lightning Source LLC
Chambersburg PA
CBHW020114310726
48970CB00002B/621